The music wa *swaying lamer* *t* *they were moving in a slow swaying* *torment.*

"So you do remember how."

Just that abruptly, amusement slid into awareness.

Heat streaked down his spine. Coiled low in his gut.

He wanted to swear.

Holding her in his arms had been a serious lapse in judgment.

Because he remembered how to do a lot of things, and every one of them was banging around inside his head, reminding him just how long it had been since he'd been with a woman.

"Remember how to smile, I mean," Lucy continued, making him wonder if he was that easy to read.

Dear Reader,

How does a person find himself or herself ready to move on after losing something—or someone—dear?

It's a question that everyone will deal with sooner or later in their life. And everyone's answer to that question will be different and specific only to them as an individual.

Time. Love. Patience. Forgiveness. To me, all of these things seem to be at least some elements of those answers. They have been to me, in any case. So, naturally, they had to be part of the answer for Lucy Buchanan and Beckett Ventura.

These two individuals meet when they are both dealing with a loss. Fortunately, they come to learn that their best answer to that question comes with loving each other.

Thank you for joining with them as they discover that taking that chance is the best chance of all.

Allison

THE RANCHER'S DANCE

ALLISON LEIGH

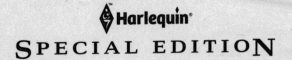

Harlequin®

SPECIAL EDITION

Recycling programs
for this product may
not exist in your area.

ISBN-13: 978-0-373-65592-2

THE RANCHER'S DANCE

This edition published by arrangement with Harlequin Books S.A.

For questions and comments about the quality of this book please contact us at Customer_eCare@Harlequin.ca.

® and TM are trademarks of Harlequin Books S.A., used under license. Trademarks indicated with ® are registered in the United States Patent and Trademark Office, the Canadian Trade Marks Office and in other countries.

www.eHarlequin.com

Printed in U.S.A.

Books by Allison Leigh

Special Edition

†*Stay...* #1170
†*The Rancher and the Redhead* #1212
†*A Wedding for Maggie* #1241
†*A Child for Christmas* #1290
Millionaire's Instant Baby #1312
†*Married to a Stranger* #1336
Mother in a Moment #1367
Her Unforgettable Fiancé #1381
The Princess and the Duke #1465
Montana Lawman #1497
Hard Choices #1561
Secretly Married #1591
Home on the Ranch #1633
The Truth About the Tycoon #1651
All He Ever Wanted #1664
The Tycoon's Marriage Bid #1707
A Montana Homecoming #1718
‡*Mergers & Matrimony* #1761
Just Friends? #1810
†*Sarah and the Sheriff* #1819
†*Wed in Wyoming* #1833

**A Cowboy Under Her Tree* #1869
††*The Bride and the Bargain* #1882
The Boss's Christmas Proposal #1940
§*Valentine's Fortune* #1951
†*A Weaver Wedding* #1965
†*A Weaver Baby* #2000
†*A Weaver Holiday Homecoming* #2015
‡‡*The Billionaire's Baby Plan* #2048
††*Once Upon a Proposal* #2078
§*The Rancher's Dance* #2110

†Men of the Double-C Ranch
§Return to the Double-C
**Montana Mavericks: Striking It Rich
‡Family Business
††The Hunt for Cinderella
*Back in Business
§Fortunes of Texas: Return to Red Rock
‡‡The Baby Chase

ALLISON LEIGH

There is a saying that you can never be too rich or too thin. Allison doesn't believe that, but she does believe that you can *never* have enough books! When her stories find a way into the hearts—and bookshelves—of others, Allison says she feels she's done something right. Making her home in Arizona with her husband, she enjoys hearing from her readers at Allison@allisonleigh.com or P.O. Box 40772, Mesa, AZ 85274-0772.

For Lanci and Bob.
May you have the lifetime
of happiness you deserve.

Prologue

Thirty-three years old.

Lucy Buchanan stared at herself in the mirror of her wholly unimpressive dressing room in the bowels of the Northeast Ballet Theater.

Although the room might have been unimpressive for all of its small, cramped size, as the principal ballerina for the company it was still hers, and hers alone.

At least it had been.

Her gaze wandered to the photographs fixed around the edges of the wide mirror. As many snapshots as there were of her and her friends at NEBT, performing, rehearsing and playing, there were just as many unrelated to NEBT at all.

Her parents. Her little brother—not that Caleb at twenty-one was anything approaching little these days. Her cousins.

Her cousins' families.

Husbands. Babies. Children.

All of the things that—after focusing a lifetime on her career—Lucy still did not have.

She avoided meeting the reflection of her own blue eyes in the mirror as she began peeling off the bits of tape that held the photographs in place. One by one, she removed the pictures, carefully sliding them into an envelope that she placed on top of the two crates that held everything else of personal note from the dressing room that she'd occupied for the better part of a decade.

Two crates that she picked up and balanced on top of each other in her own two hands.

That's what she had to show for herself.

She sighed again and shouldered her way out of the dressing room door, hitching the crates a little higher as she moved along the dim hallways. There was nobody there to bother her as she made her way through the rabbit maze toward the rear stage entrance.

The season had ended. The walls that were usually papered with rehearsal schedules and call times were empty. The three rehearsal halls echoed with silence. The rest of the company was either off to do summer touring projects or taking vacations or classes or doing the other hundred, myriad activities that dancers did to make a few extra dollars or simply just to pass the time until the season geared up again and they could return to their raison d'être.

The facility itself wouldn't close at all, though. They'd rent it out to other schools, other companies, other purposes.

When it came to NEBT's budget, the powers that be were always looking for more income to fill their coffers.

She turned the last corner and the lighting was brighter as she neared the door.

Hughes, the security guard who looked as big as a mountain but was as gentle as a mouse, looked up from the thick book he was reading when he heard her scuffling steps. "Ms. Lucy," he chided in his slow-tongued bass. "You shouldn't be carryin' anything."

She waved off his hands as he reached for her crates. "Now that I'm out of the brace, the doctor says that exercise is only going to strengthen up the knee, Hughes." So strengthen it, she would.

And maybe, maybe, there'd still be a chance she could dance.

None of which she told Hughes. She glanced at the title of the book that he'd set on the top of his desk positioned next to the rear door. "*Little Women,* eh?"

Each summer the man read every book that was on the upcoming school reading list of his only daughter. Something Lucy's own father might have done when he was raising her alone like Hughes was with his girl, Jennifer. That fact alone made Lucy think that she would miss Hughes more than most.

She smiled up at him, feeling more than a little melancholy. "What do you think of it?"

The guard grinned a little and shrugged. "That Jo is a real pip. I'm kinda hoping she gets together with that professor fella, but I think she sorta shoots herself in the foot by focusing so much on other things when it comes to that love stuff."

"True enough." She had to force her smile to stay in place. Jo wasn't the only one when it came to that sort of thing.

Hughes pushed open the door and the bright New York sunshine streamed blindingly into the stage entrance. For a moment—only a moment—she remembered the first time she'd been on stage, the brilliant lights blinding her to anything beyond the edges. Remembered, too, the thrill...

"You'll be back in the fall, right?" Despite her protest,

Hughes lifted her plastic crates out of her hands as he walked outside with her. "Be the new ballet master?"

Her smile felt even more forced. She headed toward the small car that was parked in one of the tiny lot's precious spaces and clicked the fob that hung from the flimsy ring the rental company had given her the day before. The car beeped and the rear trunk obediently popped open. "That's the plan," she said with more enthusiasm than she felt.

Ballet master. The position assigned to dancers who were either too old or too incapable of dancing themselves.

Hughes nudged aside the heavy suitcase already taking up most of the trunk space and wedged the crates alongside. "Big suitcase for a few weeks of vacation," he commented.

She lifted her shoulder, not willing to admit that the sum total of her personal possessions from the apartment she'd shared with Lars could fit into one oversized suitcase and a modestly sized shoulder tote. "You know women and clothes."

He grinned again and held the door when she opened it. "Don't mind me saying, Ms. Lucy, but that Natalia's never gonna be able to replace you."

Lucy blinked hard and stretched up to give the man a hug. "Dancers are always going to be replaced, Hughes," she said huskily. Both on the stage and—as she'd learned so well—elsewhere. "It's just the way it is." She patted his shoulder and went back down onto the soles of her flat sandals before sliding behind the wheel of the economy rental. "Enjoy the rest of *Little Women*."

He nodded and stepped back from the car as she started the engine and slowly pulled out of the lot, the sight of Hughes and the stage door in her rearview mirror.

Thirty-three, she thought again and sighed.

Might as well be a hundred and three.

Chapter One

He didn't expect her to be so small.

Beckett Ventura watched the woman from the corner of his eye as he finished fastening on his tool belt. And despite her diminutive stature, she *was* a woman, slender curves and all.

The fact that he noticed either point—short or woman—was mostly an irritation to him.

He hadn't come to the Lazy-B at damn near the crack of dawn on this particular July morning to be noticing anything at all about his neighbor's daughter.

For one thing, she wasn't even supposed to be there.

She was some fancy dancer who lived in New York and had done for years.

Or so he'd heard.

He lifted the tool chest out of the truck bed and turned toward the side of the house.

Only meant that he was also turning toward *her* because she was currently sitting on one of the front steps, her elbows on her knees as she cradled a white mug in her hands.

Of course she looked small. She was practically curled into a ball.

His jaw felt tight. Cage Buchanan, his neighbor who owned the ranch and who'd hired him for this particular job, had called him just last night. Ostensibly to check on the building project—a long-planned addition to the back of the Buchanans' two-story brick house. Beck suspected, though, that his neighbor had also wanted to let him know that his dancer-daughter was unexpectedly home for the rest of the summer.

Maybe Cage figured she needed looking after, even though he hadn't said it outright. But he had gone to the point of mentioning that she was getting over some sort of mild knee injury.

The last thing that Beck wanted was someone to look after.

He had his hands full enough looking after his daughter, Shelby. She was only six and so damn shy that she rarely managed anything above a whisper, even with her own father.

She was as different from her brother, Nick, as a person could get. Beck's son was nearly twenty-one and off at school, but he could remember him as a youngster as clearly as if it were yesterday. Where Shelby seemed shy and delicate, Nick had been all chatter and motion.

And thinking about either one of his offspring didn't make the woman sitting on the porch disappear. He couldn't walk on past her to the back of the house, much as he'd have liked to.

Wasn't neighborly, for one thing.

He had never put a lot of store in the social niceties, but

his wife, Harmony—when she'd been alive—had kept him from straying too far off the path of basic politeness.

He set his jaw and angled away from his pickup and the tin-can of an automobile with a rental company sticker in the back window that he'd parked behind. He crossed the graveled drive that ran from the front gate of the Lazy-B, circled near the house, then shot off toward the two barns set some distance away. His boots crunched across the gravel, hit the lush grass—too lush, considering it was long overdue for a good mowing—and walked toward *her*.

The fact that she was blonde was evident all along.

The fact that her eyes were as pale as the palest aquamarine, surrounded by the thickest, blackest lashes he'd ever seen only became apparent as he neared her and finally came to a stop several feet away.

She wore a skinny pink shirt with narrow straps that clung to her slender torso, baggy pants printed with pink hearts and red roses and had a scarlet colored weblike scarf looped around her arms.

She had a faint smile on her face, which was too narrow to be considered perfect. Above the scarf, the bones of her shoulders seemed ready to poke through her nearly translucent skin. Her hair—as light as corn silk—was pinned messily up at the back of her head, some of it falling around her neck.

There was no reason for him to think she was stunning.

But she was.

If he had to recognize that fact, why the *hell* couldn't he do it with the simple detachment of a person recognizing something of beauty?

Why the *damn* hell did he have to feel a jolt of heat down deep inside him where—since he'd lost Harmony—all he'd felt was a chasm of cold emptiness?

His tight jaw barely wanted to move. He gave a brief nod. "Beckett Ventura."

Her smile didn't waver. "Mr. Ventura. I figured." She set aside her coffee mug and unfolded herself from her low slouch on the porch steps. She rose smoothly, holding the long ends of the scarf together with one hand, and extended the other. "I'm Lucy. My parents told me about the construction work you're doing for them. It's very nice to meet you."

Her hand was as pale in tone as her shoulders, her palm narrow, her fingers long and slender. He might as well have been staring at a snake, ready to strike.

"Call me Beck." His voice was short and he forced himself to reach out and brusquely shake the offered hand, but only because in his head, he could see an image of his late wife, shaking her auburn head, a tsking look in her golden eyes. *Go on now,* the image spoke inside his head.

After their hands parted, he managed not to scrub his tingling palm down the backside of his jeans. Barely. "I'll try not to disturb you too much," he said evenly, lifting his toolbox a few inches.

She tilted her head slightly, those strangely pale eyes looking up at him. They would have seemed as ethereal as the rest of her if not for the ring of black that surrounded the irises, and the smudged, smoky look of her eyelashes that were oddly…sultry.

He might have grown up a hick kid from a dysfunctional ranching home in Montana, but along the way, he'd learned what women could do with cosmetics. He stood close enough to Lucy Buchanan to recognize that there wasn't a lick of anything artificial on her upturned face.

Those black, sooty lashes, so at odds with her pale hair, were all her.

"Disturb me? Are you kidding?" Her smile had widened

a little to reveal an unexpected dimple in her right cheek. "I'm so happy that my parents are *finally* adding on to this place, I wouldn't care if you made so much noise we all needed ear plugs." She didn't seem to notice his general reluctance about having to speak with her at all as she glanced over her shoulder at the house behind her. "I grew up here. My brother, Caleb, and I might have each had our own bedrooms, but there never was anything particularly spacious about the place." She sounded more matter-of-fact than complaining.

Then she looked back at him and her smile was still in place as she rearranged the scarf over those shoulders that looked as if they might break if someone handled them too roughly. "But then it was my grandparents who built it and I expect it was just fine for them." She stepped off the bottom step to the ground.

Oh, yeah. She was small. Damn near a foot shorter than he was, he figured, because the top of her head didn't even reach his shoulders. The loose pants she wore hung dangerously low around her slender hips, showing a solid three inches of bare skin below the edge of the clinging top; more than enough to see the way her hips flared out from her narrow waist.

A waist his hands could probably span with no trouble at all.

His jaw tightened again and he took a step back, moving his toolbox from one hand to the other.

It hadn't escaped his notice either that when she'd stood—for all of the smooth grace in the movement—she was heavily favoring one leg over the other.

"My parents tell me you bought the old Victor place."

He wondered what else they would have told her. That he was an antisocial widower? "Yes."

"It's a pretty property."

"Suppose." He'd just needed a piece of land on which to put a roof over what was left of his family's head since staying in Denver with all of its memories had become intolerable. Yet he'd chosen to move them all to Weaver because it had been where Harmony was born.

Not exactly moving on.

Or so his father, Stan, had pointed out more than once in the eighteen months since they'd moved into the house that Beck designed and built.

And in those eighteen months, Beck had managed to keep his interactions with everyone outside his own family to a bare minimum.

The only reason he'd agreed to the build for Cage and Belle Buchanan had been because it was July and Beck knew it was better if he stayed busy—really busy—in July. His chores around the ranch and the few head of cattle he ran just wasn't enough.

And dawdling around noticing the attributes of his neighbor's daughter wasn't staying busy at all. "I'd better get to it."

She didn't seem offended. She leaned over to pick up her coffee mug. "Let me know if you need anything."

The band of exposed skin widened fractionally.

When she straightened, he managed to move his lips in what he supposed was a reasonable facsimile of a smile. Enough so that her pleasant expression didn't change.

But as he moved away from her, he imagined he could feel those otherworldly eyes watching him go.

He waited until he turned around the corner of the brick house before he let out a breath. And waited even longer until he reached the framework of the addition he was building on the rear side of the house before he loosened his white-knuckled grip on his toolbox and set it on a stack of lumber next to some sawhorses.

"Only thing I need died three years ago," he muttered to the morning air. Two years, eleven months and sixteen days ago, to be exact.

Lucy sat back down on the porch steps and cradled the coffee mug in her hands as she watched her parents' neighbor stride out of sight.

It was just after six in the morning and the warmth of the mug between her palms wasn't quite enough to counter the cool air. It definitely wasn't enough to counter the chill that had been in Beck Ventura's eyes.

She didn't know all that much about the man except for the brief details her folks had shared. That he was building an addition for them. That he was their nearest neighbor, although he didn't socialize much.

And that he was a widower, living with his father and his small daughter.

Having met him herself, now she knew that he was tall, broad-shouldered and lean. Those chilly, painfully solemn eyes were a muddy shade of green and he had only spoken to her because he'd obviously figured he'd had to.

She hitched her scarf over her shoulders again, sipped the coffee that was still hot, even if it had stopped steaming, and stared out at the land around the house.

At least the man had picked a good place to raise his child. Lucy might have become an East Coast transplant, but she'd loved growing up on the Lazy-B. The cattle ranch had been in the Buchanan family since her father was a boy, but now at least half the branded cattle growing fat on Lazy-B grass carried the Double-C brand, which was pretty much the largest operation in the state of Wyoming. It was owned by the Clay family. They happened to be Lucy's family, too, thanks to the marriage between Lucy's grandmother, Gloria, to Squire Clay, who was the ranching family's patriarch.

Lucy still considered marrying Gloria's daughter, Belle, to be the smartest thing her dad had ever done. Not because Belle was one of the wealthy, influential Clay clan, but because she made her dad happy. One summer, Belle had come to the Lazy-B to help Lucy recover from a knee injury that had landed her in a wheelchair for months, and she'd ended up becoming the only mother who mattered.

Now, Lucy tugged up the leg of her loose pajama bottoms and studied that same knee that she'd injured yet again.

It was covered with a miserable choreography of scars. They were long and had paled over the years, having been earned when she was twelve from being thrown from a horse that had been too wild for her not-inconsiderable horse skills. But the current problem with her knee showed no scar.

Just swelling and bruises that, over the course of the past several weeks, had evolved into a putrid shade of greenish yellow.

A truck heading up the drive caught her attention. She pushed down the pant leg as she watched the vehicle race along the gravel until it came to an abrupt stop next to Beck Ventura's dark blue pickup.

She set aside her coffee again and pulled herself to her feet. "Caleb!" She'd wondered when he'd show his face.

Her brother stepped out of the truck, looking rumpled and crabby, although he slanted her a grin as he headed her way. "Hey." His voice was deep and he looked like their father, only his hair was as dark as chocolate, courtesy of Belle. "When the hell did you get here?"

"Last night. And when did you get old enough to be

staying out all night?" she asked as he caught her in a big, welcoming hug.

He set her back on her feet and grinned. "Gonna rat me out to the folks?"

"I didn't interrupt Mom and Dad's vacation to tell them I was coming home until I got here, so I hardly think I'm going to interrupt them with tales of your wild ways," she said drily. "You were with Kelly, I suppose?" Kelly Rasmusson had been Caleb's girlfriend since high school, sticking with him even when he'd left for college and she'd stayed behind in Weaver.

Caleb grimaced a little. "Not this time." He reached over to nab her coffee for himself. His brown eyes squinted as he drank down the brew. "That the rental you drove all the way from New York?" He jerked his head toward the economy car that looked particularly small situated as it was in front of two large pickup trucks.

She nodded. "I'll need to turn it in sometime this week. There's an office over in Braden." The town was Weaver's closest neighbor, about thirty miles away. And even though both communities were small, when combined, they usually provided whatever the residents needed.

"I've got some stuff to take care of there this afternoon. I can take it if you want."

She wasn't about to turn down the offer. "How will you get back if you're driving it?"

Her brother just shrugged. "I'll grab a ride from someone," he said dismissively, just as the high-pitched whine of a power tool rent the air, startling Lucy. "Beck's at it early."

A shiver danced over her skin and she hitched her scarf up yet again. She'd forgotten how chilly it could be in the mornings even in the throes of summer. "When does he usually start?"

Her brother shrugged. "Depends." He looked at the grass under their feet and grimaced. "Needed to get this mowed a week ago."

"And why haven't you?" She poked a finger into his ribs, which had him squawking and jumping to one side. "Just because it's your summer vacation from college classes doesn't mean the chores stop."

Caleb rolled his eyes. "Sounding a little like Dad, there, Luce." Still hogging her coffee, he launched up the front porch steps. "Figured all those years in New York would've knocked that outta you by now."

"Shows you're not as smart as three years of college ought to have made you." She followed him inside and closed the door. The whine of the power tool continued but more muted now. "How much longer before you finish?" He was studying pre-med.

He headed straight through the simply laid-out house to the kitchen at the rear and dumped his keys on the granite counter that had replaced the worn laminate that Lucy remembered from her childhood. "A long damn time." He drained her coffee and left the empty mug next to the keys before hooking open the stainless steel refrigerator. Another thing that had been updated over the years. As had the rest of the appliances and fixtures in the old house. Before now, her parents hadn't expanded the space, but there *had* been improvements.

She smoothed her hand over the granite and looked out the window above the kitchen sink. She could see Beck Ventura's tousled brown hair but not the rest of him.

She moved across the room.

Then she could see him properly, even though he was facing away from the house and focusing on the length of lumber he was measuring. As she watched, he shoved the measuring tape back into his tool belt, flipped the wood around with an ease that belied its awkward length, and slapped it through a saw.

Took thirty seconds, tops.

She still managed to memorize the play of muscles beneath the white T-shirt he wore and admire the economy of his movements.

Then his head suddenly turned and he looked straight at her through the window, as if he'd known she'd been standing there all along.

Her pulse tripped strangely, but she managed a smile and a wave before turning casually away again.

Only to find Caleb watching her over the leftover baked pork chop from her dinner the night before that he was eating cold from the refrigerator. "So what are you really doing here, Luce?"

"Just having a little R and R."

He didn't look convinced and his doubt helped alleviate the guilt she'd been feeling for not telling her parents all of the details that had gone into her "sudden" cross-country drive from New York to Wyoming.

If she couldn't manage to convince her little brother that everything was a-okay, there's no way on earth she could have convinced her parents.

Belle and Lucy's father had left for the vacation of a lifetime nearly two weeks earlier and before they'd left, Lucy had carefully refrained from telling them just how serious her accident had been so that they wouldn't put off their trip.

She certainly hadn't told them what had precipitated the fall resulting in her injury either.

What would have been accomplished by telling them how she'd walked in on Lars—the man she'd lived with, worked with and thought she'd loved—busily entertaining his newest protégée, Natalia, in their bed?

Knowing her father, he'd have just wanted to kill the man his daughter had been living with for the past two years.

She also hadn't told her mother that the fall that landed her in a knee brace for three weeks, putting the kibosh on her summer touring plans—as well as her status with NEBT—had occurred during her blind retreat from that particular sight. Nor had she told her mother that in those weeks since, she'd been staying with her friend Isabella, who was the company's wardrobe supervisor.

The wonders of cell phones and email. Neither of which depended upon a permanent address.

She pulled out a fresh coffee mug and focused on pouring another cup from the coffeemaker.

Did she feel guilty for keeping those details from her folks? Yes. Was there a point to lessening her guilt by confessing all to her parents? No. They'd only have insisted on canceling their six-week-long European trip that had been years in the making.

It wasn't often that Cage Buchanan voluntarily stepped away from the ranch that was his lifeblood as well as his livelihood. There was no way that Lucy wanted to be responsible for ruining it.

"My knee is doing great," she told her brother, slightly more optimistically than the truth merited. "But I had a taste for home." She glanced at him. "You know what that's like or you wouldn't spend your entire summer break here. And because I'm not working right now, might as well indulge the yen, right?"

He polished off the pork chop and licked his fingers. "Guess. You talked to anyone else since you got in?"

She shook her head. "I'll check in with Leandra and everyone later." Leandra Taggart was one of her many cousins who lived in Weaver.

"If they don't get hold of you first," Caleb drawled, because that was just as likely when word got around that she'd come home. He glanced over her head. "Looks like Beck's gonna get the rest of the framing done today."

She didn't have a clue what framing was, but she nodded anyway. "He seems nice enough." For a man whose eyes were nearly devoid of all emotion.

"Does good work, at least." Caleb opened the refrigerator door and began poking around again. "Used to be an architect in Denver."

Surprised, she looked out the window again. "Can't remember an architect ever setting up shop in Weaver before." Closest thing to it was Daniel Clay, one of Squire's five sons, who operated the only significant construction company in the area. "Is he running any stock at his place?"

"Don't think he has opened shop," Caleb said. "He just does a few building projects here and there. And yeah, he's got a few head of cattle. Enough to keep him busy when he's not doing the contractor thing." He closed the refrigerator and gave her a calculating look. "Don't suppose you've taken a cooking class or anything recently, have you?"

"Is that supposed to be a subtle way of asking if I've become a better cook 'cause you're thinking I'll start keeping *your* belly full?"

"I can only hope. Only thing you ever make are brownies and the occasional breakfast."

"Ha ha." She slid the plastic-wrapped loaf of bread that sat on the counter toward him. "Here. Peanut butter and jelly," she suggested drily. "It used to work when you were ten." She draped her scarf over the back of one of the leather-upholstered kitchen chairs and carrying her fresh coffee, started to head out of the room.

"Damn, Luce. You're walking like a cripple."

She gave him the stink eye. "Nice bedside manner, Dr. Buchanan."

He grimaced. "I just didn't realize how badly you'd still be limping. You said it was a mild sprain."

"It's stiffer in the morning," she lied. "Another month or so—by the time Mom and Dad get back, probably—I'll be right as rain."

She hoped.

Because if she wasn't, then everything she had in her life—her career—really would be over.

She deliberately turned her thoughts away from that particular pity party as well as the suspicion on Caleb's face. "Because you're being nice and taking care of my rental car, I'll take care of the grass this afternoon for you," she told her brother as she headed out of the kitchen once more. Driving around on a riding mower wasn't going to cause her knee any harm and getting out in the sunshine would hopefully get rid of the dark corners in her head. "But you can still muck out the stalls in the stable," she called over her shoulder, smiling a little because that was a chore she knew her brother dearly despised.

"Just because you're *way* older than me," his voice called after her, "doesn't mean you still get to order me around."

Her smile died as she faced the staircase that led to her bedroom on the second floor. Caleb was only joking and she knew it. But that didn't make the truth hurt any less.

Thirty-three.

She grimaced and made herself slowly climb the stairs.

Every step was agony.

As cool as it had been that morning, by the middle of the afternoon, the sun was beating down fine and true.

Lucy sat on the riding mower dressed in denim cutoffs

and a T-shirt that she'd found in her old dresser, directing the small tractor back and forth across the acre that fronted the ranch house.

Beads of sweat trickled down her spine and her muscles felt warm and loose. It was the closest she'd felt to a good workout for three miserably long weeks.

She reached the edge of lawn and turned to cut the last swath of grass in front of the house. She tipped her head back, lifting the brim of her ancient straw Resistol and narrowed her eyes against the sunshine.

She smelled fresh-cut grass, clear air and nothing but summer. At that moment, the beginning of the ballet season seemed eons away and anything seemed possible.

Even dancing? a small persistent voice whispered inside her head.

She ignored the voice and looked ahead again, tugging the brim of her cowboy hat back down to shade her eyes as she aimed toward the side of the house.

When she'd finally made her way back downstairs earlier after catching up on the phone with her grandmother and most of her cousins, there'd been no sign of Caleb, though he'd moved the mower next to the house for her from where it was usually stored in the machine shed. He'd also moved his truck from next to Beck's over to the barn.

Fortunately, some things didn't change.

As far as her brother was concerned, there was no point in walking when there was riding that could be done instead. And because there was no sign of her rental car, she assumed that he was already driving it over to Braden.

Something else that hadn't changed were her mother's flower beds that ran the width of the house. Lucy nudged the mower along the edge of them.

And that, too, felt good.

The sun. The sweat. The small details surrounding the roots of a life that still remained constant even if she'd exchanged them long ago for ballet barres and rehearsals and the heat of stage lights.

She reached the back of the house.

There was something that was not a constant.

Not the signs of expansion to her childhood home. Not the fresh foundation or the frames where new roof and walls and windows would eventually stand.

But the man who had his back toward her as he hefted an entire "wall" of studs into place.

He didn't so much as glance her way as he wielded a hammer that looked immensely heavy, nudging here, pounding there, until he reached for a nail gun that he swung around with astonishing speed.

She wasn't the only one sweating.

She could see the moisture on the back of his neck where his nut-brown hair waved into spikes. The line of sweat was working down the back of his T-shirt, making the cotton cling even more.

As she watched, he ran his forearm over his face and turned to glance at her.

Her mouth ran dry. That was all there was to it.

"Need something?" he asked loudly enough to be heard over the mower.

She shook her head. She ought to be asking him that. He was working much harder than she was trolling around on her riding mower. Maybe he needed water or something.

But getting her lips to form words seemed as impossible as it would have been for her to leap off the mower and do fouetté turns across the grass. She might be able to make her body do it, but the results would be comical at best and humiliating at worst.

His brows hitched together after her silence stretched

on a second too long, and she swallowed hard. "Looks good," she managed, and was glad that there was no way for him to know the heat in her face wasn't owed strictly to the sunlight.

He looked good. Tall. Sinewy with long, roping muscles. Oh, he definitely looked good and she was used to being surrounded by men in supremely perfect condition. Even Lars, the cheating pig, had had a perfectly sculpted physique.

Of course none of those other specimens had sported a heavy tool belt that hung around lean hips or would have even known what to do with any of the tools that it contained.

It was almost embarrassing to realize how visceral her reaction was to all that…macho-ness. Particularly when she was still stinging over the cheating pig's cheating.

In the clear sunlight, she could see that Beck's eyes weren't a muddy green at all, but a puzzle of brown and gold and green. And she was relieved when he turned the focus of them back to the construction. "It's coming along," he said.

A man of few words. She'd thought so that morning when he'd offered his almost-grudging greeting.

She wasn't all that interested in idle chitchat, either. Not even with the only person she'd met—other than the artistic director of the first ballet company who'd ever offered her a position—to make her mouth run dry. And then, she'd been nineteen and had lived, eaten and breathed ballet as if there would be nothing else in life she might miss out on along the way.

She resituated her hat on her head and began to reach for the throttle, but hesitated when he looked back at her again.

"You sure you should be doing that?" He dipped his head. "Riding that thing?"

She plucked at her leather gloves. His question struck her as being just as reluctant as his approach that morning had been and in the split second before she felt herself stiffen defensively, she couldn't help wondering if it was just her he didn't want to talk to, or people in general. "Why not?"

His gaze traveled downward from her face, making that defensiveness settle in even more. It was all she could do not to cover the ugly scars knitting across her knee. Which was pretty strange considering she'd never before felt some need to hide them. Not from her family or her coworkers or even Lars. "I'm perfectly capable of running the mower. I've done it since I was a kid."

His eyebrows lifted, as if he didn't believe her.

She grimaced. "And I've already cut the whole front side of the yard," she added.

"I wasn't saying you were incapable. Just that you looked too—"

"Weak?" She might look at the man and feel strangely weak in the knees, but she was damned if she wanted him thinking that she *was* weak *because* of her knee. She'd had more than enough of that back in New York, thank you very much. And Lord knew that she'd conquered difficulties with the joint far more serious than a bad MCL sprain.

Of course, she'd been a healthy twelve-year-old girl at the time, versus an aging thirty-three whose body was considered worn-out by the very people who'd once lauded it. "I can do anything I did before I sprained my knee." She pointed her foot as if it were wrapped in a pointe shoe instead of a dirty tennis shoe and extended her leg out almost beneath his nose.

She didn't know if it was surprise that pulled his brows together in that small but expressive frown, distaste over the old scars or colorful bruising that were in clear evidence, or irritation that she didn't succumb to her "delicate" condition but she hit the throttle anyway. Setting the mower briskly into motion again, she swiped past the neat stacks of lumber and arrangement of power tools with barely an inch to spare and sailed across the grass until she reached the far end of the lawn where a wood-railed fence separated off the corral where she'd first sat on a horse as a little girl.

Only when she reached the fence and she turned the mower to run along it did she lower her extended leg. She lifted her hat in a jaunty wave toward him, then set it back on her head and continued mowing.

Unfortunately, the pain in her leg told her she'd be paying for her foolish bravado long after Beckett Ventura was around or would even care.

As usual, her pride was definitely going before her fall. And this time, it was because of a handsome stranger with a wedding ring on his hand and a wealth of emptiness in his eyes.

Chapter Two

The afternoon had turned hot as blazes when Beck pulled his truck up in front of his house shortly before suppertime. The only things he was interested in were a cold shower, a cold beer and ESPN. Any order would work fine as far as he was concerned.

As beat as he felt, he still took the time to lock up his tools before going inside. His small parcel of land—the old Victor place, as most people around Weaver were still inclined to refer to it—was well off the beaten track. His closest neighbors were the Buchanans on the Lazy-B, and that was a solid five miles on up the road.

But old habits die hard.

A man wanted to lose tools—or anything else he held precious—in Denver, all he had to do was leave them out unlocked overnight.

He headed around to the side entrance of the house, bypassing the wraparound front porch and door that had been used only a handful of times—maybe—since they'd moved in.

He'd have happily given away every possession he'd owned in Denver if he could have kept from losing the one thing that had mattered most.

His wife.

He pushed through the wooden screen door and his sixty-year-old father, Stan, looked over from where he stood at the state-of-the-art stove. He was wearing a towel wrapped around his still-trim waist and was stirring something in a large pot with a long wooden spoon.

It was a sight that still took some getting used to considering that all through the years when Beck had been growing up, if Stan had been around at all, the only thing he'd been stirring up was trouble. Liquor-fueled trouble.

"Shelby's in the dining room," his father greeted, before turning back to the stove. "Been waiting like a little bird for you to get home so she can show you what they did at her summer camp today."

There was no point in bracing against the prick of guilt Beck felt at the mention of his daughter. Ever since her mother had died, he got that guilty feeling every single time he left his little girl. Didn't matter if he had good reason. Didn't matter that he knew she was just as happy being cared for by Stan—who'd ended up being a helluva lot better grandfather than he'd ever been a father—or at her summer day camp or even in school.

Shelby and Nick were the only things left of Harmony. His daughter deserved to grow up with a father *and* a mother, just the way Beck and Harmony had planned it from the time they'd been high school sweethearts. She deserved to have what their son, Nick, had enjoyed growing up; namely the loving attention of his mother.

Dammit to hell.

Beck *hated* July.

The rest of the year he could manage to get by without sinking too deep into the grief that never really left him.

But July?

Not even the prospect of Nick coming home for the weekend to celebrate his twenty-first birthday was enough to make the month bearable.

He shoved one hand through his hair and focused on the here and now. "What's in the pot?"

Stan gave him a look, as if he knew good and well what put the gravel in Beck's voice. "Marinara sauce. Saw the recipe on that cooking channel the other day. Figured I'd give it a go. Gonna put it on some pasta."

For the first time that afternoon, Beck felt a hint of amusement. Spaghetti noodles had become "pasta" since Stan had taken up watching the pretty female chefs on television.

Most of Stan's "give it a gos" were on the fair side of mediocre, but he was happy and willing to keep them in food so Beck and Shelby were happy and willing enough to let him. "Sounds good."

"Guess we'll find out," Stan said wryly. "Lord knows Nick'll tell me plain enough if it's not when he gets here tomorrow night." He gestured with his spoon and a splotch of red sauce landed on the granite counter. "Don't forget Shelby."

As if Beck would. He veered away from the back staircase he'd been aiming for when he entered the house and headed through the kitchen to the dining room instead.

His daughter was perched on one of the chairs, sitting on top of two old telephone books that raised her up enough so she could reach the table better. Her walnut-brown head was bent over the papers spread across the glossy wood surface of the long table. She heard his footsteps and her eyes—Harmony's golden eyes—looked up at him, then swiftly shied away.

She might have been waiting for him just as Beck's father claimed, but it was still a hell of a note when his own daughter was shy with him.

Which left him feeling like he was always walking on eggshells around her. "Hey, peanut. Whatcha drawing?"

Her narrow shoulders hunched. "Pictures." She leaned closer to the table, as if she wanted to hide whatever it was she'd been wanting to show him.

Since the moment they'd lost Harmony, Beck had missed his wife. But the times when he missed her most were in the morning when he'd first wake up and think—just for a split second—that his life was still complete and he could turn his head and find her laying beside him. And times like now, when he was with Shelby, wishing like hell that Harmony was there to help him be the kind of father their daughter deserved.

He slowly pulled out the chair next to his baby girl and sat down. "Pictures of what?"

Her shoulder hunched again. She was wearing a light pink shirt with dark pink flowers on it and for a second— only a second, he assured himself—an image of Lucy Buchanan danced in his thoughts.

She'd been wearing pink that morning, too.

And that afternoon, when she'd been driving that damn riding mower all over creation.

He touched the corner of one of the large pages. "Can I see?"

"I guess." Shelby's voice was only a shade above a whisper. But at least this wasn't a habit she reserved only for him. Last year, her kindergarten teacher had repeatedly told him that she was trying to get Shelby to speak up in class.

"Is that you?" He pointed at the stick figure in the center of the page that sported a shock of brown hair and a pink dress that was about ten times too wide for the body. There was a house behind her and an enormous sun taking up an upper corner of the page.

"Uh-huh." Showing a little more animation, Shelby rested her elbows on the table, leaning forward.

He got a whiff of baby shampoo and sweet little girl that made him hurt inside.

"We hadda draw what we wanna be when we're growed up," she confided. "Annie Pope only drew one picture, but I hadda draw three."

Annie was Shelby's friend from kindergarten. And it was Annie's mom who'd suggested that Shelby might enjoy going to the daily afternoon camp.

"Why three?"

"'Cause I don't know what I wanna be yet."

"Well," he considered that seriously, "that sounds fair to me." He'd look at a hundred pictures a day if it kept his daughter talking to him. "So what are you in this picture?"

She gave him a strange look, as if he ought to be able to decipher it for himself. "A mommy." She jabbed her finger against the page. "I'm holding a baby. Can't you see?"

"Oh. Right." His daughter didn't know how her words sent a pain through him. She'd been barely three when Harmony had died. "I see that now."

She pushed the paper aside, fussing with the other sheets of paper until they were just so. "Annie drew a horse," she said under her breath. "She can't grow up to be a horse." She giggled.

Beck smiled. His fingers grazed the ends of her hair where it lay in an untidy sheet down her back. It was still as soft as silk. He glanced from her face to the pages on the table. "And this one?" He nudged one of the pages, sporting another stick figure with the same brown hair, this time accompanied by a dozen smaller stick figures.

Again, he earned another "duh" sort of look that he figured he'd be receiving plenty of the older she got. "A teacher."

Meaning the mini-sticks were her students. "Okay." He angled his head to get a better view of the last page.

And for some reason, he knew straight off what that drawing was.

Maybe it was the jagged-edged crown that sat atop the brown hair. Or maybe it was the stick arms that were thrown up above the crown. Or maybe it was because the thing Shelby liked pretending to be most was a ballerina.

"A ballerina," he murmured.

"Mmm-hmm." Shelby leaned completely forward until her chin was resting on her hands atop the table, with her nose only an inch from the drawing. "That's the best one. Grandpa says we'll hang 'em on the 'frigerator so Nick can see 'em when he comes home."

"Sounds like a plan." Beck tousled her hair. He wondered what Shelby would think if she knew that a real ballerina was hobbling around right next door. Not that he intended to make a point of telling her. Shelby would just end up fascinated, and the dancer would just end up leaving to go back to her normal life. The last thing his daughter needed was anyone else leaving her. "Grandpa will have supper ready soon. Go wash up your hands."

"Okay." She was back to a whisper and he stifled a sigh as she obediently slipped off her telephone books and chair, grabbed Gertrude, the hand-stitched rabbit that her mother had made before Shelby's birth, and hurried out of the room.

He scrubbed his hand down his face, his gaze on the ballerina drawing.

He didn't want to be reminded about Lucy Buchanan.

Not by his daughter's drawings and certainly not by his own thoughts.

She'd been in pain.

That fact had been as visible as the swelling and faded scars had been on her leg.

That incredibly…lithe…shapely…leg that seemed much too long for someone so small.

He pinched his eyes closed, forcing the image out of his head before shoving back from the table.

Too bad he couldn't forget about that pain she'd been suffering.

It nagged at him through a cold shower, when he pulled on a clean pair of cargo shorts and a T-shirt afterward, and particularly when he sat on the side of his bed and picked up the framed photograph that sat on the floating shelf beside it.

Harmony's face stared back at him.

His wife had always found the best in people, even when there wasn't a lot of "best" to be found. He was a perfect example of that. She also couldn't have turned a blind eye to someone's pain even if she'd wanted to.

Harmony hadn't been just the name that had graced his wife. It had been *who* she was.

He'd learned that when he'd met her when he was sixteen years old.

He'd been the local drunk's son who preferred getting in fights over trying to make friends. Who failed classes for the sheer pleasure of flouting his teachers' efforts.

She'd been the new girl in school who didn't look at him with pity in her eyes. And when she'd sat down beside him at lunch one afternoon, ignoring the silent warning that screamed from his pores and smiled that smile of hers, he'd been a goner. Two years later, barely out of high school, she'd been pregnant with Nick and they'd eloped.

He rubbed his thumb over the photograph, as if he could still feel the thick ends of her vibrant hair.

But the only thing his thumb felt was cool, smooth glass.

Echoes of the angry kid he'd been still lingered in the man he'd become. He'd lost his wife and the harmony she'd created in his life. And no matter how badly he wanted to, now he couldn't even recall exactly how it had felt to run his fingers through her hair.

He pushed the frame back onto the shelf and stomped downstairs. Shelby and his dad were already sitting down to their dinner plates, which were situated around the breakfast bar in the kitchen rather than the dining room's long wood-planked table that Beck had commissioned from a wood artist he knew back in Denver.

When he'd packed up his family, he hadn't packed up the house he'd shared with Harmony.

Every stick of furniture that she'd chosen to fill the home he'd built for her had been left behind. Sold off or given away by the company that Beck had hired the day he'd realized that staying in that house without his wife was going to be the end of him.

He ate the spaghetti, which was better than usual, and watched Shelby suck in noodles through her pursed lips and giggle at her grandpa when he did the same.

Just another night in the Ventura household.

There was no reason—other than the looming anniversary of his wife's death—that Beck should feel like he was ready to climb out of his skin.

But he did.

And before either his daughter or father had finished

eating, he was pushing back from the breakfast bar. "And you think there's plenty of leftovers, even considering Nick's appetite when he gets here?" He headed toward the stove to look into the pot. Typically enough, it still held a whopping amount. Stan might have developed a penchant for cooking, but he still figured he might as well be expedient about it and get at least a few meals out of each effort.

"Yeah." Stan supped another string of spaghetti into his mouth, every bit as messily as his granddaughter was doing.

Beck left them to their amusement and rooted out a clean plastic container from the mess in one of the cupboards and began filling it. When it was practically overflowing, he fit the lid on top and headed toward the door.

"Going to feed the homeless?" Stan asked dryly.

"Just the injured." He glanced at his father. "I'll be back before Shelby's bedtime." His daughter's lashes quickly lowered before she could get caught looking at him and he stifled a sigh as he went outside.

His father caught up to him before he could slide into his truck, though. "Where are you going?"

Beck set the container of food on the seat beside him. "I forgot something over at the Buchanan place."

Stan's brows shot up. "Since when do you forget anything?"

Since he couldn't remember the feel of his wife's hair under his fingertips.

Beck turned the ignition. He got along well enough with his father now—again, thanks to Harmony's efforts—because he recognized that Stan *was* a good grandfather. Unquestionably helped by the fact that Stan had stopped drinking by the time Nick was out of diapers and hadn't touched a drop since. And once Beck was on his own, left behind to his drowning grief and a three-year-old toddler to raise, Stan had become even more entrenched in their lives when he'd stepped in to help. He'd taken care of Shelby and hadn't commented at all while Beck found his own way out of a bottle.

"Since today." His voice was short as he reached for the door. He grimaced. "I won't be long."

Stan stepped out of the way of the door, and pushed it closed himself. "I'm guessing you met the daughter."

"What?"

"Heard she was back when I was picking up Shelby from day camp. Everybody was talking about seeing her at Colbys last night just before closing time. Said she was practically dragging when she went inside and ordered up whatever was still hot in the kitchen."

"Did they." Beck's voice was dry, but inwardly—considering how he'd seen her favoring her leg—he figured *dragging* was probably a pretty accurate telling. More accurate than the usual gossip that was always rife in small towns like Weaver. "I met her in passing."

"And now you're taking her food," Stan added, as if he couldn't believe what he was seeing with his own two eyes.

"Maybe I just don't want us all to be eating *pasta* for the next four days," Beck returned. "You cooked enough for an army."

"No point in cooking for one meal when it's no more work to cook for two."

Beck just shook his head. "Don't forget to pin up Shelby's pictures on the fridge," he said, and put the truck in gear before his father could say anything else.

Twilight was beginning to settle as he drove the narrow road that led to the Lazy-B, but Beck had made the trip often enough that he knew every pothole, bump and sudden curve—daylight or not—and the spaghetti was still hot in the container when he pulled up in front of the Buchanan place twenty minutes later.

Only once he was there, looking at the simple lines of the old brick house that were outlined against the deepening sky, did he start wondering what the hell he *was* doing there.

The Buchanans were related to the Clay family and even as antisocial as he was, he knew their numbers were plentiful in the area. If she needed looking in on, she had plenty of family who could do it.

He pinched the bridge of his nose.

The dancer had left the front door open, probably to take in the air that had begun cooling once the sun started heading toward the horizon, and he could see past the screen straight back through to the kitchen.

He swore under his breath because now that he was there, it seemed worse than stupid to turn around and go home. So he grabbed the spaghetti and stomped up to the front door.

He lifted his hand to knock, but that's when he glimpsed the damnably familiar sight of a long leg stretched out against the staircase.

His nerves bumped and instead of knocking, he grabbed the handle on the door and pulled. The lack of a lock wasn't surprising considering how far out in the boondocks they were, and he strode inside, his mind already casting around to remember what he'd ever learned about first aid.

But instead of an injured woman collapsed on the stairs, he got a glimpse of wholly startled blue eyes as Lucy— perfectly conscious even if she *was* sitting on one of the steps about three-fourths of the way from the top—gaped at his intrusion.

"Beck!" She whipped the thin folds of her pale gold robe

over her legs and wrapped her hand around the banister next to her head. "What on earth are you doing?"

Making an even bigger ass out of himself. "I thought you'd hurt yourself."

She went still, her gaze flickering for a moment. "Thank you for the concern, but as you can see, I've done nothing new." Her hand tightened around the banister and she pulled herself up to her feet in one smooth motion that seemed to belie the fact that her knee was injured at all.

Except that Beck had seen the way her knuckles went white before she so much as budged an inch.

He set the spaghetti container on the narrow table that stood against the wall and moved to the foot of the stairs. "If it's so bad, why bother going up and down the stairs in the first place?"

Her lips—a little too wide for her narrow face—parted softly. And just as quickly they were pressed into a thin line. "It's not that bad. And my bedroom is upstairs," she added as if it should be obvious.

He snorted and planted his foot on the bottom tread before reaching up to grab her waist. Ignoring the hiss she gave, he lifted her right off the stairs and carried her the few feet to the living room.

"I don't appreciate being lifted around," she muttered as he deposited her on the couch there.

He could still feel the suppleness of her waist and the slick silk of her robe against his palms, but he managed a bland look. "You're a professional ballet dancer. Don't you get lifted around all the time?"

"That's hardly the same thing." With a quick tug, she tightened the belt around her waist and flicked the robe over her legs again. The thin fabric floated down to settle over her bare feet.

He still managed to notice they were narrow, high-arched and her gangly toes were painted a pale pink, and it irritated the hell out of him.

He wasn't interested in anyone's toes, for cripes' sake.

"I *was* managing just fine," she said, evidently oblivious to his foot ogling.

"That was pretty obvious," he drawled as he moved across the room to retrieve the spaghetti. "Where's your brother?" He hadn't seen Caleb's truck where he usually parked it near the barn. Not that Caleb had been spending much time at the ranch, as far as Beck had noticed over the last few weeks since he'd started construction.

Protests or not, now that she was on the couch, she didn't look in any hurry to move when she leaned her head against the cushions behind her. "He turned in my rental car earlier and then he went back into town."

"Is he coming back?"

The pale, pale blue was a narrow sliver between her dark lashes as she sent him a look. "He's a big boy. I'm sure he can find his way home when he's ready." She lifted her slender hand. "And I didn't come home wanting him—or anyone else in my sometimes-interfering family—assigning themselves as my babysitter."

"Maybe you should have," he said bluntly, "if you can't get yourself up and down the stairs." He held up the plastic container. "My father sent over some supper." The lie was preferable to the truth.

Not that he was even all that sure *what* truth had propelled him back to the Lazy-B that evening.

"I *can* get up and down the stairs," she defended. "And that was very kind of your father but hardly necessary."

He shrugged and headed into the kitchen. "Just being neighborly. And you haven't seen the army that my dad thinks he's cooking for," he said as he went. He'd been inside the Buchanan house more than once; mostly because there was no getting around Belle when she was insistent about something like inviting him in for lunch or coffee whenever he had met with Cage for one reason or another. But he still had to open a few cupboard doors before he found the plates. He dumped out a healthy portion on one, stowed the rest in the plastic container inside the nearly barren fridge, hunted a little more for some silverware, then carried everything back out to the living room.

He extended the plate toward her. "You'll hurt his feelings if you don't eat." Another guilt-free lie. Lifting her off her feet had been about as taxing as tossing a pillow. As far as he was concerned, the dancer could stand to eat more. A lot more.

She took the plate but didn't look all that happy about it. "Again, that's sweet of him, but I *can* fend for myself."

"Okay." He reached to take the plate back from her, but she let out a laugh that was as unexpected as it was quick, and held the plate out of his range.

"I'm also not foolish enough to turn down a meal when it's looking me in the face." A smile hovered on her lips, revealing that faint dimple again. "Particularly one I didn't have to cook for myself." Her lashes lifted for a brief moment as she glanced up at him. "Are you going to hover there while I eat, or sit down?"

He'd done what he'd come to do. Deliver the food and put an end to the annoying niggle in his head that hadn't let him forget the bravado she'd shown earlier that day on the mower. False bravado.

The pain in her face then had been as plain as the white knuckles she'd needed to stand up on the stairs.

Her brother wasn't around to watch out for her, but she had food in her hands, a couch under her rear. Beck had even noticed the cell phone that was sitting on the end table, within easy reach, which meant she had a passel of family, too, within easy reach.

No reason for him to keep hovering, that was certain.

But his feet made no move toward the door.

He swallowed another oath, even as he found himself sitting down on the couch beside her.

And then he wished that he'd at least had the sense to sit on the chair that was adjacent to the couch.

He looked away from the vee of smooth skin that extended from her long neck down between the lapels of her robe where they criss-crossed between her breasts.

Legs that seemed strangely long for someone so short, and breasts that seemed strangely full for someone so slender beneath the skim of that pale gold silk. The fabric was only a shade darker than her skin.

He realized he'd lifted his hand to run it around the too-tight collar of his T-shirt and curled his fist.

It was July for God's sake. The anniversary of his wife's death loomed like a specter over every breath he drew.

What the hell was he doing noticing—*really* noticing—the attributes of his neighbor's daughter?

He started to push off the couch but went dead still when she reached out and closed her hand over his arm. "Wait."

When was the last time a female had touched him?

He'd barely had the thought before her hand moved away again, returning to steady the plate that she was balancing on her lap.

"Sorry." She focused on the fork she was swirling into the spaghetti. "It's just a drag to eat alone."

There was a rosy glow on her high cheekbones that hadn't been there before. His need to escape battled something else.

The something else won, and he subsided on the couch. "I s'pose. I haven't eaten alone in a long time."

She paused, her laden fork aloft, as she gave him a quick look. "You live with your father and daughter?" The spaghetti disappeared into her mouth.

He realized he was staring, and not entirely because the mouthful she'd taken had been enormous.

This particular dancer wasn't exactly eating like a bird. Her appetite looked as healthy as his.

"Yeah," he answered a beat too late. "We're all usually together when it's mealtime." He wished he'd have been as careful with that point when his wife had been alive.

Lucy swallowed and her tongue snuck out to lick the corner of her lips.

His appetite gave a low, rumbling growl and it had nothing to do with food.

His fingers drummed on the upholstered arm of the couch as he felt an urgent need to escape. The opened front door wasn't doing a good enough job of allowing the cooling air inside. He abruptly pushed off the couch. "You need something to drink with that."

"You don't have to wait on me."

But her voice was following him because he pretty much bolted toward the kitchen.

The glasses were in the cupboard next to the plates. He got one down and turned on the water faucet. Looked over his shoulder through the doorway.

All he could see was the back of her blond head. The hair that she'd had twizzled up that morning in a messy clip and that had been mostly hidden beneath her raggedy cowboy hat that afternoon was now down, pooling over the couch cushion behind her head, looking as pale and soft as moonlight.

Water spilled over his hand, cooling the twitch in his

fingers that seemed to know, instinctively, how soft those strands would be even though they'd been unforgivably forgetful about what his *wife's* hair had felt like.

He shut off the water, wiped his hand on his shirt and carried the glass into the living room. He set it on the coffee table in front of her, then took the seat adjacent to the couch.

Lucy toyed with her fork, trying not to watch Beck too closely. She feared that if she did, it would spook him. And even though she wasn't sure she wanted any company at all—not when her knee was throbbing so badly it made her feel ill and long for the pain pills that were in bedroom upstairs—she felt reluctant to do anything that would cause him to bolt.

"Your dad's a good cook." She lifted a bite to her mouth again, feeling only a twinge of guilt for what was an unusual gluttony of carbohydrates.

"Sometimes." Beck's lips twitched faintly, and Lucy realized that she had yet to see him actually smile. "But he's always better than me, so we're happy."

She reached forward to retrieve the water glass and instinctively knew the moment that his gaze shifted a little. It happened at the very same moment that she felt the lapel of her robe loosen and gape slightly as she leaned forward.

She was no exhibitionist.

So there was no reason for her to sit up more slowly than she should have. No reason at all.

But that's exactly what she did.

She sat up slowly, tucking her loose hair behind her ear as she did so. She didn't know how much she was revealing as the silk lapels tightened again against her chest, and that *not*-knowing was sending nearly as much warmth through her veins as his suddenly sharp gaze was.

But once she was sitting upright once more, his gaze had

moved circumspectly back to her face—or at least around her face, because his eyes didn't meet hers. But her breath still felt strangely short, and the brush of her robe against her nude skin felt strangely erotic.

She sipped the water, not entirely sure whether she welcomed the attraction or not.

Until she knew whether her knee would fully heal or not, she was stuck in a holding pattern. Unable to move ahead and make a life that might be wholly different from everything she'd ever worked for. Unable to move back and regain control of the life that she'd had. Either dancing again if she was very, very lucky, or at worst, accepting that being NEBT's ballet master was simply the next stage in her life as a dancer.

Whether she appreciated her attraction to Beck or not, her blood was humming in her veins in a way it had not for a very long time—even before Lars's defection—and her nipples were so tight they were nearly painful. The kind of painful that was only assuaged by a man's touch.

Beck's touch.

Her gaze had dropped to his long-fingered hands, and realizing it, she felt a flush bloom hotly across her face.

She quickly lifted the water glass and drained it. "So, uh, how long have you lived in Weaver?"

"Year and a half."

"Caleb said you're an architect? From Denver?"

He nodded once.

Didn't offer any elaboration. Didn't make any attempt at all at conversation, for that matter.

She wasn't used to feeling tongue-tied or out of her element. She was usually comfortable around most people; could usually find something to talk about with anyone, whether they were reporters or ballet patrons or strangers on the street.

She looked at Beck Ventura, who still wore a wedding ring despite the fact that he was widowed, who had chilly shadows deep inside his eyes, and all she had were questions that she didn't feel comfortable asking and an attraction that she was fairly certain was returned. And even more unwanted on his part than it was on hers, judging by the expression on his face.

She wished she hadn't finished off the water so quickly and moistened her lips. "So, what brought you from Denver to our little old town of Weaver?"

A fresh shadow came and went in his eyes. He looked toward the doorway as if he wanted to get to it just as badly as she'd wanted to get to the pain pills that she hated being weak enough to need, before her knee had simply given out while she'd been climbing the stairs.

"My wife was born here." His answer was as abrupt as the way he suddenly pushed himself out of the chair. "I need to get home." He didn't look at her as he headed toward the door, only to stop halfway there. "Do you need anything?" The question was almost dripping with reluctance, but something about the way he waited told her that he wouldn't go until he had an answer. An honest one.

She thought about the bottle of pain pills that she'd been pretty darn intent on getting to earlier, when her regular dose of over-the-counter hadn't done the job.

"I'm fine," she said quietly. Sincerely. Because she'd finally figured out what was behind that cold solemnness in his eyes.

And what was a bum knee in comparison to a broken heart?

Chapter Three

Lucy knew that it wouldn't be long after her arrival before the rest of the family began descending on her.

For one thing, she might as well have announced she was back by megaphone while standing in the center of town considering that she'd stopped in to Colbys Bar & Grill the night that she'd arrived in town.

There was one sure way to get gossip started in the town of Weaver, Wyoming, and that was to show your face in the most popular watering hole on Main Street.

And even though she'd touched base with most of them on the telephone the morning before to assure them that she was fending for herself quite well at the Lazy-B, they soon started arriving.

First came her grandparents bearing coffee and over-size sticky cinnamon rolls that they'd picked up at Ruby's Café on their way through town from their home on the Double-C ranch.

Gloria and Squire Clay technically weren't Lucy's grandparents. Gloria and Squire had been married for as long as Lucy could remember, but Squire had already raised five adult sons by that time, and Gloria had raised Belle and her twin sister, Nikki. And Belle was Lucy's stepmother. But those kinds of distinctions had never mattered when it came to the family that her father had married into.

To the Clays and everyone who came under their umbrella, family was family. Love was love.

It was that simple.

So Lucy swallowed her protests that she was fine and didn't need them worrying about her and let Gloria, who was a retired nurse, fuss over her knee and let Squire, who'd become an unrepentant and somewhat wily nosy body in his later years, guilt her into eating not only half of one of the decadent rolls, but the whole darned thing.

Spaghetti the night before.

Fat, fluffy cinnamon rolls now.

She'd be working out for hours just to calm her conscience.

Then, before Gloria and Squire departed, one of Lucy's cousins, Sarah Scalise, showed up with her three kids in tow.

The house just got more crowded as the morning wore on.

And even though Lucy was truly delighted to see each and every one of them, she couldn't help but be aware of the silence from the back of the house where the day before had come the sound of Beck's power tools and hammer.

He hadn't shown up that morning at all.

Because of that strange, stilted dance they'd conducted over his mercy package of spaghetti? Or because of something that had absolutely nothing whatsoever to do with her?

A part of her chided herself for thinking that *she* might have had any disturbing effect on the man strong enough to make him keep his distance. But another part of her knew that…disturbing…had definitely been one of the things floating in the air between them.

"So, we'll all meet at Colbys tomorrow night," Sarah was saying as she stood in the doorway, keeping a weather eye out on her two thirteen-year-olds—Eli and Megan—as they kept their four-year-old brother, Ben, occupied in the front yard. "Girls' night out." She'd already made plans with the rest of the cousins to meet in town. "We'll catch up on all the gossip and drink until we're silly and my husband's deputy sheriffs will have to drive us all home." She grinned. "Sound good?"

"Sounds great." Lucy had a smile on her lips because she *was* looking forward to it, but she also knew her gaze kept straying past her cousin to search the road for signs of a dark blue pickup truck.

"Sure you don't want me to come out and get you?" Sarah lived in the town proper, whereas most everyone else lived in the outlying rural areas, like the Lazy-B.

"I drove here all the way from New York," Lucy reminded her wryly. "I think I can make it into town from here."

"And I still can't believe that you rented a car to drive it," Sarah returned. "It would have been so much quicker to fly."

Lucy shrugged. "I like to drive." She was not averse to flying, but she'd needed the long hours on wide-open roads to get her head together and shake off the worst of her feelings about what she'd left behind.

In one part, she'd been fairly successful.

She could think about the cheating pig, for example,

without wanting to break something. Namely his handsome face.

In another part, however, she had accomplished nothing. Because she was no closer to knowing what to do with her life if she couldn't go back as a dancer than she had been when she'd packed up her dressing room at NEBT.

As she left, Sarah was still shaking her head as if she couldn't fathom Lucy's decision. "See you tomorrow evening," she called as she corralled her kids into her SUV.

Lucy nodded and waved, and even after her cousin was long gone, she kept checking the road for signs of Beck.

Eventually, she told herself she was being ridiculous and made herself stop. She'd dressed in her usual workout clothes—stretchy camisole and dance pants—when she'd finally made it up the stairs that morning. After having slept on the couch all night with her knee elevated on a pillow, it had settled down so well that she'd been able to go up and down the stairs with very little difficulty at all.

She filled a water bottle, grabbed her cell phone and headed across her freshly mowed grass toward the old barn that was situated closest to the house.

It was there that her father had put together a virtual at-home rehab unit when she'd been twelve, and the very basic notion of walking again had been nearly out of reach. All of the equipment was still there, situated in a partioned area that consumed half of the barn's space along with a portable dance floor that she'd had installed herself nearly ten years ago. Neither were exactly state-of-the-art, but everything was perfectly maintained and perfectly serviceable for Lucy's purposes.

There was a boom box that was as old as she was stored on the shelves that her father had built, alongside fat, folded tumbling mats and towels that—when she plucked one off the stack—smelled freshly laundered.

Which meant, she thought with a vague smile, that Belle was probably still using the barn as a workout space. Her father had never needed to use equipment or weights to stay in shape, not when he had an entire ranch as his workout arena.

She plugged in the boom box, popped in a random CD from the stack of them on the shelf and dragged down one of the thick mats, flipping it out in the center of the floor in front of the mirror that lined one wall.

Then, with the sound of some New Agey music that Belle must have chosen filling the lofty space, Lucy got down to work.

It was the music that got his attention. More specifically, it got Shelby's attention, which meant that Beck couldn't just ignore it because he figured it was coming from the dancer anyway.

He somehow doubted that Caleb Buchanan was the one responsible for the lush orchestration of some classical music that his mind recognized even if he couldn't identify the composer.

It had been a hectic morning, not helped by the fact that the leader of Shelby's day camp had come down sick and cancelled the day. And Stan had an AA meeting over in Braden that he attended every week on Friday mornings, after which he was driving down to Cheyenne to pick up Nick, who was flying in that afternoon from Princeton.

The second Beck parked the truck where he usually did near the house, Shelby hopped out, clutching Gertrude the rabbit. Like a dog scenting game, his daughter jerked her head around as she listened for the source of the music. "What's that?"

"Sounds like music to me." He grabbed the bag of books and toys he'd pulled together to keep her entertained, then lifted his toolbox from the truck bed and went around the truck to her. "Come on." He touched the top of her silky head. "I'm working around the back of the house."

Once he had her situated in the shade nearby, he figured he could get in at least a good hour or two before the afternoon was spent. The trick, he knew, was to make sure Shelby stayed occupied. Because once she got bored, there was no way he'd be able to get any real work accomplished.

"It's coming from over there," Shelby whispered. She was squinting into the sunlight as she pointed her finger toward the older of the two barns.

The only reason Beck knew what the barn contained was because half of the building supplies he'd ordered for the project were stored there until he'd need them.

He had an image of Lucy hobbling her way from the house over to the barn and felt his nerves tightening up.

He set the toolbox and Shelby's bag on a stack of lumber, and took his daughter's hand. "Come on."

She gave him a startled look, but hurried to keep up with him as he strode to the barn.

The door was pushed open to the warm afternoon, and as they stepped through, the music was so loud that it was almost deafening.

And his heart damn near stopped in his throat when he saw Lucy sprawled face down, unmoving, on one of the wide blue mats that had been spread out atop the dark gray floor that took up most of the space.

Curses floated inside his head. He should have had the presence of mind to keep Shelby at bay. He let go of her hand. "Stay here." He didn't wait for any more of an answer than her widening eyes, before he strode across the springy floor.

He reached Lucy's side and crouched next to her. Memories of the day he'd found his wife collapsed in their home crowded his mind, making his stomach churn and his hand shake as he reached out to touch the back of that blond head. "Luc—"

Her head whipped up, her hair flying out around her back. Her pale blue eyes were clearly startled. "Beck!"

Relief froze him into place. His heart climbed back out of his throat. Nausea seeped away.

And all that was left was anger.

"Goddammit, Lucy," he cursed softly. "What the hell are you doing?"

"Working out," she said and her voice had turned just as chilly as her eyes. "Not that it's any of your business." She pushed up to her hands and knees and he could see the sheen of sweat on her face and her chest above the low scoop of her clinging pink shirt. A sheen that was echoed on her bare shoulders and arms.

"Working out?" He nearly choked. "Last night you couldn't even make it up a staircase."

Her lips tightened. "That was last night." She straightened her knees beneath her, sending her rear end—perfectly displayed in body-molding black pants that ended around her ankles—up in the air, and with her hands still planted on the mat in front of him, stretched. "And if you don't mind, I'd like to finish my stretching." She lowered her head and the long, thick strands of her nearly white hair slid over her shoulders to coil on the mat between her hands.

He scrubbed his hand down his face and sat back on his butt. Images swirled inside his head. Harmony, racked with pain that he couldn't alleviate as her eyes begged for release. Lucy, lithe, slender and golden, as she watched him with those otherworldly, sultry eyes.

And now that body was on display in a clinging fabric

that assured him that even though she was thin, that thin-
ness was comprised of perfectly sculpted flesh. Lean.
Strong. Female…

"Daddy?"

He jerked, feeling like a damn kid caught staring at
something forbidden, and Lucy's head whipped up again.

He was used to his daughter's half-whispered voice,
was always attuned to it. But how Lucy heard it above the
music was something else.

She straightened slowly and the blue of her eyes warmed
as she spotted his pint-size daughter.

She sent Beck a questioning look before she moved
across the mat and hit a button on a large, outdated boom
box. The music ceased and the silence that came after it
seemed almost as deafening. "Who is this?" she asked. She
walked toward Shelby, her gentle question clearly meant
for his daughter.

Shelby was staring wide-eyed at Lucy, her stuffed rabbit
clutched protectively to her chest.

Beck shoved to his feet.

Despite the pain he'd seen on Lucy's face the previous
day, the way she was moving now told him that his worry
had been for nothing.

She moved as smoothly as water flowing over rocks.

And watching her was just as mesmerizing.

Dammit.

"This is my daughter. Shelby." He headed toward her.
"And we'll get out of your hair."

Lucy gave him a thin look and deliberately stepped behind his daughter, neatly cutting off his exit. Then she bent
her knees until she was on Shelby's level. "I'm Lucy." She
stuck out her hand as if she were meeting an adult. "And
it's very nice to meet you, Shelby."

Shelby blinked a little, then shyly extended her own

hand. Lucy's smile widened, revealing that dimple again, as they shook. Then she tugged on the rabbit's fabric ear. "And who is this?"

"Gertrude," Shelby answered so promptly that Beck nearly did a double take.

"Hello, Gertrude," Lucy greeted the rabbit and shook one of the faded paws. "I'll bet you and Shelby are the very best of friends."

Beck's gut tightened again. "Come on, Shelby. I've still got some work to do before Grandpa gets back with Nick." He held out his hand and his daughter obediently tucked her narrow fingers into his. He sidestepped around Lucy.

"You're here to work?" Lucy straightened again, somehow managing yet again to block his exit.

"What else would I be here for?"

Her gaze flickered, and his head filled again with the way she'd felt the night before when he'd carried her to the couch.

The way she'd felt.

The way she'd looked.

And the fact that he *had* looked, just as he did now.

His hand tightened around Shelby's. "Come on, peanut."

"Wait." Again Lucy stopped him. "What's Shelby going to do?"

His jaw was so tight that it felt like his molars were grinding to dust. "She has her books and toys."

"She could stay here with me," Lucy suggested, clearly not swayed by his abruptness. Her gaze slipped away from his to look at his daughter. "We could get to know each other." She smiled at Shelby.

"She'll be fine with me." He took another step, but the resistance tugging at his hand was so unexpected that it penetrated even his urgent desire to put some distance between him and the disturbing woman.

He looked at his daughter. She was clutching the rabbit with her other hand and her lashes lifted enough to peep up at him. "I wanna stay."

His molars were definitely grinding together.

It was a wonder all three of them couldn't hear it.

"Lucy's doing her own…work," he said. "And she doesn't need to be playing babysitter."

Shelby's lashes swept down again. The corners of her lips turned down.

"*Lucy* can say well enough what she wants to do," Lucy countered smoothly. "I've already offered." She swept her hand above her head, then down to her side as she lowered into a small—and definitely goading—plié. "And my *work,* as you say, is pretty much done for the day."

He didn't want to agree.

It wasn't particularly logical. He didn't begrudge Shelby spending time away from him. She went to school. She went to her summer day camp. She had even—on a few rare occasions—spent the night at Annie Pope's house.

But he didn't want her spending time with Lucy Buchanan.

He looked from the glint in Lucy's eyes to the disappointment in Shelby's. And felt, too, the resistance in Shelby's hand.

How often did his daughter actually express what she wanted?

He let go of her little hand. "Fine." He didn't let himself look back at Lucy. It was obvious that the woman wasn't in danger of physically collapsing and he would be within shouting distance no matter what. "For an hour," he warned his daughter, cutting short the time he'd planned to work and not caring one whit. "And then we'll go home and see Nick."

Shelby's eyes widened and looked up at him again. She nodded wordlessly.

He turned away, only to stop dead when Lucy's hand closed over his bare forearm.

"Thank you."

He didn't want her thanks. He damn sure didn't want to feel his nerve endings coming to life beneath the feather-light touch of her warm palm.

It was July.

The only thing he wanted was to feel as little as possible, to survive the month the best he could and endure another year without his wife before July rolled around yet again.

He shifted and Lucy's hand fell away.

The nerve endings still didn't stop dancing their annoying jig.

"If she gets to be too much, yell."

Lucy's smile didn't waver. "I'm sure that won't be the case." She gave a quick wink toward Shelby.

His painfully shy daughter was clearly fascinated.

He wished he could be happy about that.

"An hour," he said again, and then he walked out of the barn.

Lucy bit back a sigh as Beck stomped away, but when she looked down at his daughter, she made sure none of her unsettled feelings about the man showed on her face.

"So, Miss Shelby. How old are you?"

The little girl's narrow shoulders hunched a little. "Six." The answer was so soft that Lucy had to bend closer to hear.

"Six." She held out her hand and couldn't help feeling a little triumphant when Shelby took it with much less reserve than her timid expression indicated. "So what grade does that put you in? Sixth?"

Shelby shook her head emphatically. "Sixth is for the big kids. I'm *little*."

"Ah, I see," she said seriously. "Then you're going to be in…kindergarten?"

"No! First."

"Of course." Lucy pressed her hand to her chest. "Silly me. Maybe I need to go back to school myself!" She tilted her head toward the exercise equipment and the mats. "So do you want to come into my playroom?"

Shelby nodded.

They padded across the springy mats and Shelby kicked off her little white tennis shoes as they went until she was as barefooted as Lucy was and Lucy grinned. "Do you like music?"

Again, a nod.

Lucy pulled down a handful of CDs from the shelf. What did she have on hand that would appeal to a six-year-old girl? "Do you know what kind you like?" There wasn't any Hannah Montana or whatever it was that little girls wanted to listen to these days, but there were some soundtracks from old Disney movies.

Shelby suddenly reached up and pushed Gertrude onto the shelf where the boom box sat and punched the "play" button. Rachmaninov immediately blasted again through the barn. "I like that," the little girl said clearly.

Lucy laughed and turned down the volume. "Well, okay, then." She brushed her finger down Shelby's straight nose that was a miniature version of her father's. "Sweetheart, you and I are going to get along just fine."

And Shelby smiled.

Thank goodness at least *one* member of the Ventura family hadn't forgotten how.

* * *

"Another round, ladies?" Their server at Colbys stopped next to Lucy the next evening and glanced around the crowded table.

There were seven of them in all because even her cousin, Angeline, who was about ready to pop with the baby she was carrying, had driven over from Sheridan with her family for the weekend. Seven and not a single man among them.

After all, it was a girls' night. No men allowed.

"Count me in," Lucy told the server and was quickly echoed by the others.

The server grinned as he collected their empties. It was a combination of martini glasses, beer bottles, sodas and water; as varied as the women clustered around the table. Some were cousins. Some were spouses of cousins.

And all of them were friends.

Lucy watched the server work his way through the bar. It was Friday night and the place was as crowded as she'd expected it to be. "Who *is* that kid?" she asked in general. "He looks familiar to me."

Leandra laughed and leaned her blond head across the table toward Lucy. "He ought to. That's Mark Strauss. Scott Strauss's baby brother."

Lucy winced. "Baby is right," she muttered. She'd gone out with Scott Strauss a few times in high school and his little brother had been just a toddler then. "This getting old business is for the birds."

"I don't even want to hear the word *old*," Sarah interjected. She was sitting next to Lucy. "Yesterday, Eli told Max that he wasn't going to ever get married until he was old like we were." She gave a mock shudder. "Talk about out of the mouths of babes."

Lucy couldn't help but laugh. Sarah was a year younger

than she was. And even though her husband, Max, was more than a decade older, he hardly fit the definition of "old." The guy was the local sheriff, and as hard and handsome and fit as sin.

For that matter, every one of the women she was with had won the lottery when it came to seriously attractive husbands—both outwardly and inwardly. Lucy was the only one at the table who wasn't married with a growing family.

And just then, as much as she loved them all, that fact made her feel like the sore thumb. "When is Courtney supposed to get here?" Of all the women Lucy counted among her cousins, there were only a few who weren't married. Courtney was one. She was a registered nurse and only twenty-five. The rest were even younger—from early twenties all the way down to three.

Lucy's family, no matter the generation, was nothing if not prolific.

"Courtney said she was switching shifts at the hospital," Mallory offered. She was an obstetrician and had become the latest addition to the Clay family when she'd married Lucy's cousin Ryan, who was also Courtney's brother. "She's still on nights."

"Well." Lucy eyed Angeline, who was leaning back in her chair. She had her hands folded over her enormous belly and still managed to look beautiful with her exotic South American heritage. "I guess if Angel there goes into labor, it'll be good we've got an O.B. with us. Once Court gets here, we'll have a whole medical team."

Angel gave her a lazy glare. "I'm due in two weeks. I am *not* having the baby this weekend. Brody would never let me live it down. I had to use all of my feminine wiles to get him to agree to drive us up in the first place."

J.D.—who was as blonde as her sister Angeline was

dark—snorted. "It figures that *you*, who are about twelve months pregnant, would still have some wiles left to wield."

Angeline eyed J.D. "As if you and Jake weren't doing the horizontal up until the last minute before Tucker came along?"

"Probably all that hot, sweaty sex is what brought on the premature labor," J.D. agreed, grinning wickedly, and they all laughed. Tucker had come early—very early—which had been a worry for everyone, but the infant was making up for his slow start with astonishing speed.

Then the Strauss boy returned, doling out their second round of drinks before taking their food orders, which not surprisingly, were as eclectic as their drinks had been. Courtney arrived soon after, and then their party was complete. Lucy just sat back and absorbed their laughing, easy company.

Yes, she did miss all of this when she was away.

Her fingers toyed with the stem of her wineglass as her gaze drifted from their faces around the bar. A familiar brown head had her stiffening, though.

Sarah noticed and glanced over, too. She leaned her head closer to Lucy's. "Got a problem with your folks' builder?"

"Not at all," she answered swiftly, looking away from Beck as he made his way through the crowded bar toward a table across the room.

He was with two other men. Judging by the strong resemblance, Lucy figured the older one was his father and the younger was the Nick that Beck had mentioned. Thanks to Shelby's chatter during the much-too-brief hour that Lucy had gotten to spend with her yesterday afternoon, she'd learned that Nick was Shelby's big brother.

But Sarah just gave Lucy a look, and she exhaled. "I

don't know what to think of him, okay?" Except that he didn't make her feel old and past her prime.

Not at all.

A wicked smile was toying around Sarah's lips. "Which means you *are* thinking something at least."

Lucy rolled her eyes. "I just got out of one relationship. I'm hardly interested in starting up something new. Consider me currently off men." Because she'd had to or face their wrath, she'd already admitted to them that Lars had chosen someone else over her. Although, as with her parents, she hadn't tied that particular point with her sprained knee. Nor had she admitted that her career was hanging by a thread.

"Off *all* men might be overdoing it, but when it comes to Beckett Ventura, it's probably just as well," Sarah murmured. "That is one seriously grieving man. Half the single ladies—and a few attached ones, so I've heard—have thrown themselves at him and he never even blinks."

Lucy hesitated. Her gaze kept straying toward him. He was seated at a table on the other side of the room and she didn't have a clear view. "Do you know what happened?"

"With his wife?" Sarah shook her head sadly. "A coworker of mine had Shelby in her kindergarten class last year. Evidently his wife died of cancer a few years ago. Shelby was only three. Deirdre told me it sounded as if Beck moved his family, lock, stock and barrel away from their home only a few months later."

He might have moved, but from what Lucy could tell, he hadn't moved *on*.

"Anyway, if you're looking to get over Lars, our Mr. Ventura is probably not the way to go," Sarah murmured.

"Speaking of…have you heard from Lars since you left?" Angeline asked.

Lucy shook her head. "Nope. According to my friend Isabella—she's the wardrobe supervisor—" she added for Mallory's benefit "—he's *very* busy with the lovely Natalia." She grimaced.

"Lars was an ass," J.D. said bluntly, jumping back into the conversation. She pointed the tip of her fork in Lucy's direction. "And not worth a minute of your grief. Best thing for you is to jump back on the horse." Her lips twitched. "So to speak."

"Is sex *all* you ever think about?" Angeline asked blandly.

J.D. just smiled and shrugged. "Do you disagree with me?"

Which had everyone rolling into more laughter when Angeline had to admit that she didn't.

Shaking her head at all of them, Lucy pushed up from her seat and brushed down the folds of her gauzy sundress. She didn't want to think about sex. Mostly because her thoughts, irritatingly enough, went immediately in the direction of the grieving Beck. "I'll be back."

Turning sideways, she worked her way through the tables toward the restroom in the rear of the room. She could see Beck's table as she went, though his gaze never turned her way.

She wondered where Shelby was. She wondered if Beck would manage to find a smile now that his son was home for a visit. She wondered *why* she couldn't stop wondering about the man.

There was a line at the ladies' room, and by the time she returned to her table, the crowd around it had suddenly doubled. Girls' night out had been duly crashed by a horde of husbands.

Not that Lucy could spot a speck of unhappiness on anyone's face. And once the hugs and the kisses were out of the way as the husbands welcomed her back to town, more tables were dragged together, more chairs were crowded in, more drinks and more food were ordered.

It was hectic, it was chaotic, it was loud and boisterous. It was Friday night at Colbys. It was home.

And later, as couples began drifting off—to the dance floor to grab a romantic moment free from babies and kids, to the pool tables to grab back bragging rights, even to other tables to catch a word with an old friend—Lucy sat at the table with her foot propped on an empty chair and soaked it all in.

When she was in New York, she'd felt like she was home. When she was here? She felt like she was home, too.

But which one *was?*

She toyed with the stem of her wineglass and her eyes drifted over the bar. It was more crowded than before, though the families who'd brought kids to eat in the restaurant were being replaced by young adults—most on the obvious prowl.

"Refill?" She glanced away from the dance floor to the Strauss boy and shook her head. "I'm good, thanks." He quickly moved on and when he did so, Lucy found herself looking straight at Beck who'd come up behind the server.

Her nerves went as tight as piano wire.

There was no use pretending that he'd just happened to notice her. Their tables weren't on the way to anywhere. Not the exit. Not the restroom. Not the long bar itself.

His gaze focused on her leg stretched over the chair between them, the folds of her dress hiding her knee. "Overdoing it seems to be a habit for you."

The fact that he was right didn't mean she had to acknowledge it. Instead, she lifted her wineglass and the pale chardonnay that still filled the bottom of it glistened. "Good evening to you, too, Beck."

His lips twisted and he looked away as his hand closed over the wooden back of the chair. "Looks like they've all abandoned you."

"No more than you've been," she pointed out. His son, Nick—a thinner, younger version of him—was dancing with Courtney. His father—a shorter, slightly stockier version—was dancing with Susan Reeves who'd arrived along with her nephew Jake, who was J.D.'s husband.

Beck gave a silent faint nod, acknowledging the point.

She sipped her wine, studying him. Up until now, she'd only seen him wearing T-shirts and worn jeans and tool belts. Tonight, though, he wore a beige button-down shirt that her experienced eye recognized as silk with black jeans and polished boots. He looked casual, sexy and as comfortable now as he did when he was hefting around power tools and lumber that weighed nearly as much as she did.

And just as disturbing.

She drew her leg off the chair. Thanks to the icing she'd given her knee before she'd come into town and the dose of aspirin, it wasn't as painful as it had been earlier that day. For which she was grateful. It was bad enough knowing she'd pushed too hard the day before—again—without letting that fact show to Beck. Again.

"Would you like to sit down?" It seemed only polite to invite him, which didn't explain at all the way she held her breath, waiting for him to shake his head and move on.

He shook his head. Only he didn't move on.

He lifted his chin toward the dance floor. "I thought maybe you'd rather be out there."

She hesitated, surprised. "Are you asking me to dance?"

His lips thinned again. "I thought about it." His gaze

skimmed over her. "Not that I figure you ought to be, considering your bad knee and all."

Something inside her stomach skittered around.

He looked like he wished he'd kept his mouth shut.

So naturally she set down her wineglass and pushed to her feet. "Well, then," she said sweetly. "How could I possibly turn down such an irresistible invitation?"

As if it were the most natural thing in the world, she wrapped her hand around his wrist, pulling his clamped hand away from the chair and headed toward the dance floor.

Chapter Four

He should have cut out his tongue.

But now it was too late.

The dancer was turning against him, putting one hand on his chest and drawing his other—the one she was holding—around to the small of her back. She tilted back her head to look up at him and her river of blond hair tickled his arm. "Where's Shelby tonight?"

He didn't know what he'd have done with his hand if she weren't still holding it in place behind her, but he was pretty certain it wouldn't have involved lingering there, absorbing how delicate—how feminine—that faint hollow felt. He stared at the mirror that hung on the wall behind the bar. "Spending the night with her friend, Annie Pope."

"Ah. She mentioned Annie. Evidently she wants to be a horse?" She smiled slightly.

He knew because he saw it in the mirror.

Hell. Might as well be looking at her face if he was going to watch her anyway.

"She also told me her brother was home for his birth-day?"

"For the weekend, yeah. He flies out again tomorrow night. He's taking classes over the summer."

"Good for him. Must be a hard worker."

He glanced at his son. "He's a good kid."

"How old is he?"

"Twenty-one as of today." He still found it hard to be-lieve.

"Ah." Her dimple flashed mischievously. "Out for his first drink?"

Beck made a face. "His first legal one anyway. He *is* in college."

Her smile widened. "What's he studying?"

"Architecture."

"Following in your footsteps," she observed. "Makes a father proud."

He didn't take credit for Nick's successes. That was owed as much to Harmony as it was to him.

"I have to say you don't really look old enough to have a grown son," she continued.

"Feel old enough," he murmured.

She moistened her lips, looking strangely discomfited. "Do you, uh, like country music?"

"Only thing I've ever heard playing here."

Her eyebrows rose. She finally let go of his hand behind her back, which was good.

But all she did was loop her two hands loosely around his neck instead.

Which was bad.

He stared over her head again and wondered what the hell he was doing.

"That wasn't exactly an answer," she pointed out after a moment.

"It's music," he said evenly. "It's as good as any other."
Right now the song was going on in a slow, swaying lament
which only meant that they were moving in a slow, swaying
torment.

"In other words you don't give a rat's patootie."

He looked down at her, catching the amused glint in her
eyes. He felt his lips tilt. "Not really."

She blinked and suddenly looked away. "So you do remember how."

Just that abruptly, amusement slid into awareness.

Heat streaked down his spine. Coiled low in his gut.

He wanted to swear.

Holding her in his arms had been a serious lapse in
judgment.

Because he remembered how to do a lot of things, and
every one of them was banging around inside his head
reminding him just how long it had been since he'd been
with a woman.

"Remember how to smile, I mean," Lucy continued,
making him wonder if he was that easy to read.

"Yeah." He cleared his throat. "I remember." The song
ended, moving seamlessly into another, and he stepped
back as the beat picked up. "That's it for me," he said.
"Thanks."

She said nothing as he backed away. Just watched him
with those pale eyes that seemed to see too much.

Like the fact that he was escaping, pure and simple.

Nick had moved on from the statuesque blonde to a
petite brunette, and his father was still sticking close to
the Reeves woman. Neither one noticed when Beck aimed
straight for the exit.

Outside, he sucked in a deep breath of fresh night air.

The music from inside the bar was muted only slightly.

He shoved his hands through his hair and sat down on the bench that faced the empty street.

He sighed and stared down at the wedding ring on his hand.

He'd hawked his beater of a car when he was eighteen to buy their plain gold wedding rings, and twenty-one years later, he was still wearing it.

Aside from a wristwatch, it was the only jewelry he'd ever worn. He curled his hand into a fist. For so long the ring had been as much a part of him as the finger it circled.

"You all right?"

He jerked and looked up.

Lucy was standing beside him, holding two longnecks in her hand.

"You make a habit of sneaking up on men?"

Instead of being put off by his terseness, her lips curved faintly, though not really with amusement. "Apparently so." Her voice was mild and she held out one of the beer bottles. "Want it?"

He wanted lots of things, most of which began and ended with a grave in Colorado. If he hadn't had Nick and Shelby to consider, he'd have come close to climbing in one, too.

But he hadn't. And he was here. And an annoyingly appealing woman was standing nearby, filling his senses with more life than he wanted to acknowledge.

But he unfisted his hand and closed it around the cold bottle anyway. "Drinking on a public street's probably frowned on around these parts."

"Probably." She twisted open her beer and sat down beside him. "But I've got family connections to the sheriff." She softly clinked the bottom of her bottle against his. "No worries."

Even if she didn't have connections, what was the worst that would happen? He'd get a ticket?

Small potatoes in the scheme of things.

He opened his own beer.

And they sat there in silence for several minutes while the muted music from inside throbbed through the wooden bench beneath them.

He stared at the park across the street. There were some kids chasing each other around and their carefree laughter floated on the air.

"There's a pavilion over there in the park where the teenagers go to neck," she said. "At least they used to when I grew up here."

He didn't look at her. It had been so long since he'd carried on a conversation having nothing to do with his family or work that he could practically taste the rust. "Did you?"

"Neck? Sure. A few times." She held the bottle loosely between her fingers and swirled it around a little.

He noticed, though, that she didn't drink much of it.

The beer had just been an excuse.

To come out here.

With him.

Knowing it was one thing. Knowing what to do about it was another. And he wasn't even going to touch how he felt about it with a ten-foot pole.

"I'm sorry about your wife, Beck."

He went still.

Dozens…maybe even hundreds…of people had offered the same sentiment over the past three years. His employees at the architectural firm that he'd walked away from. His friends. His family. Even near strangers. He should be used to hearing it by now.

God knows he'd gotten used to saying the usual "thank you" and moving on as quickly as possible.

Instead, the words that he heard coming out of his lips weren't usual at all. "I loved her."

His jaw tightened and he stared even harder at the park across the street. He couldn't see the kids over there anymore. Maybe they'd gone to the pavilion. Maybe they'd just gone home.

"That's the way it should be." Lucy's voice was soft. Wistful.

He looked over at her. She was watching the park, too, her long hair streaming over one slender shoulder.

"What do you want from me?"

He knew what his body wanted from *her*—something he had no intention of indulging which was why it was better all around if he stayed away from her. He hadn't cheated on his wife when she was alive. He wasn't sure he was ready to do it now either.

But he was still a man. With the predictable reactions around an incredibly sexy woman.

But women? They had different things that drove them. He'd figured out one woman in his lifetime. Wasn't that enough for one man?

The last thing he wanted to do was start wondering what exactly drove *her*.

He didn't want to be interested, but no matter how hard he tried to pretend he wasn't, he was.

"What do I want?" Lucy's head slowly turned. Her eyes met his. "I don't know. Maybe just to see you smile again. A real smile. The kind that stretches all the way across your face."

He stretched his lips into a humorless smile. "Satisfied?"

She didn't look offended. "Not yet." She took a brief sip

of her beer and looked back out at the park. She stretched out her injured leg and pointed her toes, flat thin-strapped sandal and all, then lowered it again. It seemed such an absent motion that he wondered if she even knew she was doing it.

At least it was easier to focus on that curiosity than it was on the unwanted attraction nagging persistently at him, reminding him that his heart might be dead, but the rest of him was not. "You grew up here, didn't you?"

"On the Lazy-B?" She nodded. "Yup. Loved it, too."

"How'd you end up being a dancer?" There was no dance school in Weaver now—he knew because it was one of the few things that Shelby had actually complained about to him. But maybe there had been a studio when Lucy'd been a girl.

"I took lessons. Not in Weaver," she allowed, as if she'd been reading his mind. "My dad had to drive me miles and miles for them." Her lips curved. "Usually griping all the while."

He knew Cage Buchanan. The guy was devoted to his family. "I doubt it."

Her smile widened. "Okay, maybe he complained only some of the time." She stretched out her other leg and pointed her toes. "But it all paid off. Dancing was always my dream. My parents helped me make it a reality."

"And now ballet's your life."

She lowered her leg again. "Right." She lifted her beer bottle. Took a longer pull. Stared across the street. "Everything I ever wanted was in the ballet," she murmured softly.

Then she let out a breath and shook her head a little.

He eyed her profile. It wasn't perfectly in balance. Her narrow nose turned up a little too much at the end. Her chin had a little too much of a stubborn tilt.

And when she was lying—and he was pretty sure that she was—the right corner of her soft lips turned down. "What's wrong with your knee?"

"Sprain." She hesitated a moment. "A pretty serious one."

"It'll heal?"

She nodded. Less hesitation this time, but something about the way she held her shoulders made him wonder.

"And then you'll go back to New York," he concluded. "How'd you sprain it?"

She lifted her beer bottle again, only to look at it for a moment and lower it again to her lap. "By falling down the stairs after I found my boyfriend in our bed with another girl." She gave him a quick look and rolled her eyes, looking embarrassed. "I don't know why I told you that."

"Is it true?"

She let out a silent, humorless laugh. No curving down at the corner of her lips at all. "It's true all right." She grimaced. "I just haven't told anyone else that's how I ended up like this." She swished the fabric covering her knee.

"Who was he?"

She didn't answer for a moment. "The choreographer and artistic director for the ballet company I danced for."

He didn't know a lot about how ballet companies operated but he could make a guess. "Probably makes it hard to work with him now."

She tilted her head, acknowledging. "Particularly when he replaced me as the principal ballerina with *her* as well only a few weeks earlier."

"Guy sounds like an ass. Messing around where he works?" He shook his head.

"Mmm." She shifted. "That's not entirely fair of me, though. I don't know if you can liken the ballet world to most other things, but it's pretty much a hotbed of drama.

And whether I like it or not, Lars was doing his job. Doing the best thing for the company. I'm thirty-three." She lifted her shoulders and grimaced. "It's not as if I expected to keep the position forever. Much as my pride would like to think otherwise."

Thirty-three looked pretty prime to him, but admitting it aloud didn't seem like a very smart move. Not when he was doing his best to ignore that particular fact. "What does that mean for you, then?"

"No longer being the star of the show?" Her shoulder brushed his as she lifted her beer bottle. "It's just a hitch in the road," she dismissed. Her gaze glanced off his again. "How long were you married?"

He wasn't sure if they were in some sort of verbal dance or sword play. She clearly didn't want to talk about her career any more than he wanted to talk about himself. He could end it, simply enough, by getting up and walking away.

His butt stayed planted right where it was, though.

"Eighteen years." He knew he sounded irritated, but it was directed a lot more at himself than it was at her.

"That's even longer than I've been a professional dancer."

"Don't sound so surprised. My son turned twenty-one today. Yeah, it was a long time." He flexed his jaw that had gone tight again. "It should have been longer."

She said nothing. But after a moment, her hand settled lightly on his arm.

He didn't brush it off even though warmth ripped through him.

And they continued to sit there until his beer bottle was no longer cold beneath his fingers and his father finally came looking for him.

"Been looking for you for a half hour," Stan said and

didn't bother trying to hide his curiosity as he looked from Beck to Lucy and back again.

Beck stood. "I got tired of watching you flirt with Susan Reeves," he returned. "Where's Nick?"

"He's still inside with that pretty little brunette. Tabby, I think her name is."

"Tabby Taggart," Lucy provided. She stood, too, only to gasp and pitch toward Beck as her knee gave way.

He caught her and his pulse skyrocketed as he took her weight against him.

"Sorry," she muttered breathlessly. Her hands pressed against his chest. "Guess I'd better work on that balance or I'll be pirouetting off the stage when I get back to New York." She laughed lightly as she stepped away from him and moved around the bench. "Tabby Taggart," she said again. "Your son shows good taste. She's a nice girl. Her brother's married to my cousin. Evan Taggart. He's a vet. Has an office not far from here." Switching her virtually untouched beer from one hand to the other, she extended her right one toward Stan and introduced herself. "You're Shelby's grandpa," she added quickly.

Too quickly to Beck's mind.

She was flustered.

Because she'd stumbled? Or because she'd stumbled against him and with that full-body contact had realized what sort of state *he* was in?

"It was really kind of you to send Beck over with the spaghetti the other evening," she was continuing. "I should have felt guilty making such a pig out of myself eating every bit of it, but it really was delicious."

"My pleasure," Stan assured, though he gave Beck a telling glance.

"I, um, I'll be sure to get the container back to you soon." She was scooting toward the entrance of the bar.

"I'd better get back to my family." Without looking at Beck again, she sketched a quick wave and slipped inside the door.

"Well," Stan said after a deliberate pause once she was gone. "That was interesting."

"Don't start."

"She's quite a looker."

Beck eyed his father.

Stan tossed up his hands. "Fine. Fine. I won't remind you that you've still got a life to live."

Beck only stared harder because, of course, that's what Stan had just done. And over the past year or so, those reminders had been coming more frequently.

He moved around the bench, heading for the door, too. "It's late. I'm going to get Nick."

"You think this is what Harmony would want for you? She made you promise to move on, remember?" His father followed him.

Just as he always had before, Beck ignored the question.

But as he worked his way through the bar, looking for his newly "officially adult" son, his eyes strayed toward Lucy.

She was standing next to a pool table where one of the teachers he'd seen at Shelby's school was pushing her long red hair behind her slender back before lining up a shot. As if Lucy had felt his attention, she looked over her shoulder at him.

The skin on his forearm went warm, as if she'd reached out to put her hand there again, and he deliberately looked away.

Yeah, he'd always ignored Stan's nagging about moving on.

It had never been difficult.

But tonight, it was.

The weekend passed with no sign of Beck at the Lazy-B.

Not that Lucy had expected him to come over and work when his son was home to visit, or even to work on the weekend, for that matter.

But she still found herself watching for his truck. Listening for the whine of one of his power tools.

It was a good thing, then, that she hadn't spent a whole lot of time at the ranch herself. Not when her grandparents decided to throw a barbecue on Saturday at the Double-C that lasted until the wee hours. And then, on Sunday, she drove back into town again to attend church.

She rarely went to church in New York.

But get home to Weaver? Then it was just the thing that people did.

Weaver had a few churches. More now than they'd had when she was growing up because the town had easily doubled in size since then. She knew that Beck didn't attend the same service she did. One, because she didn't see him. And two, because Sarah, who'd been sitting behind her, had leaned over Lucy's pew to whisper—sounding like innocence personified—that Beck didn't attend there at all.

Which meant she spent most of the service listening with half an ear while wondering if he went to *any* church.

She wasn't exactly being the model worshipper, she figured, and diligently tried to listen more closely to the sermon.

But it was hard because the good reverend was preaching about loving thy neighbor.

Then after church was Sunday dinner, which the

extensive Clay family always held every week at one or another's house. Didn't matter how many people could make it. Those who could, did. Those who didn't, usually made it the next week.

It was tradition. And going there felt right to Lucy, too, even though it meant another round of concerns expressed about her knee.

This time, the meal was at Ryan and Mallory's place. They had a seven-year-old daughter, Chloe. Which only reminded Lucy of Shelby, who was a year younger.

By the time Monday morning rolled around, she had to face the fact that even when the man was out of sight, he definitely wasn't out of mind.

Didn't seem to matter that she was perfectly aware of his grieving. Didn't seem to matter that she knew focusing on anything other than getting herself back in dancing form was most likely just another way of not dealing with the uncertainty of her future.

Whether he liked it or not, he was attracted to her.

That particular fact had been more than apparent.

Equally as apparent as the fact that he didn't want to be.

When Beck hadn't shown up by the middle of the day—about the same time that Caleb finally showed up from wherever he'd been all night—she was a bundle of nerves from waiting.

She'd mucked out half of the stalls in the stable, leaving the other half for Caleb.

Fair *was* fair after all, and even though she took pride in being capable, shoveling horse manure wasn't exactly high on her list of favorite things to do, particularly when it took her three times as long to do it because her knee kept giving her fits.

She'd also mopped the floors, cleaned the kitchen and baked a triple batch of chocolate brownies from scratch.

All to keep from hovering in the front window watching and waiting...

For a woman who was supposedly "off men" she was showing all of the signs of being *on*.

"Smells good." Caleb wandered into the kitchen, obviously freshly showered because he still had a towel wrapped around his neck. He leaned over the large sheet pan that she was dolloping swirls of icing over.

"Don't touch." She swatted away his hand.

"Hey." He gave her an injured look. "I just wanted a taste. What's the occasion?"

"I'll give you a taste when I'm finished. And there is no occasion."

His eyebrows went up. "Lot of brownies there. You planning to go on a major binge or something?"

She deftly lifted out a square for him and set it on a napkin.

He promptly shoved half of it in his mouth.

She grimaced. "You're the one looking like a pig. I figured I could take them to Sunday dinner." And maybe next door to the Venturas. It would only be neighborly, after all, to return the favor of the spaghetti.

Her brother was grinning as he swallowed. "Think they'll even be around by the end of the week?" He tucked the remainder in his mouth and went to the refrigerator where he pulled out a jug of milk and poured it straight into his mouth.

"So this is what college has done for you? Made you forget *all* of your manners?"

His grin only widened and before she could stop him, he'd scooped another soft, sticky brownie right out of the pan. "I'm heading out." He turned to leave the kitchen. "Don't wait up, Grandma."

"You better not be doing anything stupid like drinking and driving when you're staying out at all hours with Kelly like you have been," she called after him.

He glanced over his shoulder at her and the grin was gone. "Who says I'm with Kelly?" Then he took another bite of brownie and disappeared, leaving Lucy blinking.

She went straight to the telephone and dialed Sarah. "Who is Caleb dating?"

"Kelly Rasmusson, of course. Why?"

Lucy licked the chocolate frosting from the end of her thumb. "Just curious," she dismissed, although she was more curious than ever what company her baby brother was keeping these days. "Max still have a soft spot for homemade brownies? I made a huge batch and I'm willing to share."

"My husband has a soft spot for anything chocolate," Sarah said with a laugh. "And the only time *you* turn on the oven is when you're stressed out. So, what gives?"

"I turn on the oven," Lucy defended.

Sarah laughed again. "When?"

"When I have to," she allowed, then laughed a little herself because Sarah was right. If Lucy could find a way around cooking or baking for herself, she usually did. "I have to run into town anyway tomorrow morning, so I'll bring some by for you."

"What's tomorrow?"

"Dr. Valenzuela is driving up from Cheyenne to see me. We're meeting at the hospital." The renowned orthopedist was one of the same doctors who'd treated her when she'd been a teenager, and he still worked for her uncle Alex at the sports clinic located in Cheyenne.

"Ah. Checking on the knee?"

"Yeah." Lucy drew her fingertip along the edge of the brownies, gathering up another taste of icing.

"So *that's* the reason for the stress," Sarah concluded. "I knew there had to be something, but sort of thought it might have something to do with your widowed neighbor."

"I am *not* stressed."

"Whatever you say," Sarah soothed, clearly disbelieving. "Eli!" Her voice went sharp. "Do *not* bring that muddy dog in this house. Gotta run, Luce. See you tomorrow."

The line went dead and Lucy hung up the phone.

Along with returning to all the comfortable, familiar things she loved, coming home also meant being among people who knew her too well.

She washed her sticky hands and arranged a dozen brownies in a container. Then, before she could do something really foolish—like go upstairs again and fuss with her hair or her clothes as if she really were trying to impress someone when her knee was already protesting all of her activity that day—she retrieved the keys for one of her father's ranch trucks and left the house behind.

She'd been on the road to the old Victor place often enough when she'd been growing up and as she drove it now, she figured it hadn't changed much.

It was still rutted and narrow and winding and more than once, she had to catch the brownie container from sliding off the seat beside her. But the moment she turned off the road and drove through the stone arch that marked the entry to the small spread, all she encountered was change.

It hadn't really dawned on her that Beck Ventura had money. The kind of money that went well beyond the purchase of a small parcel of Wyoming land.

She blew out a silent whistle as she drove along the smooth, paved road that was bordered by tall lilac bushes and acres and acres of rolling grassland on which a few head of cattle were grazing. The lilac bushes had been there for years, she recalled. Overgrown. Untended. Now, they were trimmed and glossy and once they were in bloom, she figured it would be a spectacular sight as a person approached the house itself.

And what a house it was. Two stories. A covered porch that ran the entire front of the dwelling. Two wings that extended on either side. It was large without being too large and even though it had a distinctly rustic flavor—which she considered in keeping with the setting—it still managed to seem elegant. Gracious.

More evidence of money, although not in any ostentatious way. She recognized it, having seen the signs herself in the homes that the various members of the Clay family had built in the area over the years.

She slowly rolled to a stop in front of the house and climbed out of the truck. She couldn't see any other vehicles near the house or the low-roofed barn that was the only original building from the Victor place that seemed to be still standing. She certainly didn't see Beck's truck.

Maybe he wasn't even there.

Which was probably exactly all that she deserved.

Chewing the inside of her lip, she went up the low steps and crossed the porch that had been furnished with chunky, dark-wood furniture and had barely lifted her hand to knock on the massive door when it was yanked open.

Beck stood there wearing jeans and a denim shirt with a black cowboy hat on his head. His dark expression was wholly unwelcoming. "What are you doing here?"

Her stomach jerked around and her nerves quailed.

Annoyed, she lifted her chin and forced her gaze upward from the denim covered chest in front of her. She held out the containers. "Being neighborly," she said pointedly.

"Returning your container and bringing brownies for your father and you and Shelby as well."

A muscle twitched in his angled jaw as he looked down at her offerings. Then he exhaled roughly and stepped back. He didn't verbally invite her in, but the faint jerk of his head seemed to be one, so she moved past him into the house.

"Lucy!" A bullet in the form of Shelby skidded in stockinged feet across the hardwood floor, and Lucy didn't even have enough time to brace herself against the little body as it pelted against her.

Beck's hand behind her back, though, did the trick.

It also made the skin between her shoulder blades feel as if it had been branded. She couldn't even jump away, though, because between his implacable hand and Shelby's body, she was stuck.

She smiled down into the little girl's face and tried to ignore the warmth of the man behind her. A futile endeavor if there ever was one. "Hey, there. How are you today?"

"We didn't have day camp." Her voice was back to her usual near-whisper, but that didn't lessen her dramatic passion as her thin shoulders rose and fell. *"Again."*

"Bummer. So what did you do instead?"

"I drew pictures in my room. Wanna see?" She stared up at Lucy with such a mix of shyness and hope that it made her ache a little inside.

Lucy balanced the containers in one hand and gently tucked a strand of hair behind Shelby's ear with her other. "Absolutely," she assured softly.

But even as she did, Beck's dismay seemed to form around her like a visible cloud. He didn't voice his protest, though, and took the plastic containers from her when Shelby grabbed her hand and led her toward the staircase that curved grandly into the foyer.

Lucy hid a grimace when she reached the base of the

daunting flight and started to follow the child up. Unfortunately, by the time she'd made it halfway to the landing, she was sweating from the effort of not favoring her sore knee.

A quick glance down to the foyer told her Beck was still there watching them. Even from the distance she could tell his eyes were narrowed. Could feel the waves of his disapproval.

She didn't have any desire to upset him. But she also had no desire to dim Shelby's excitement.

She still remembered how it had felt before Belle entered their lives. How it had felt to be motherless.

It didn't matter how much she knew her dad loved her. She'd wanted a mom.

And short of that, she'd wanted the attention of a grown woman. Nearly anyone would have done.

"My room's up here, Lucy." Shelby was nearly bouncing on her feet where she was waiting on the landing.

Six more steps to go.

She reminded herself that she'd managed much worse in her time. She tightened her hand around the banister and started climbing again, never mind trying to save face by moving naturally.

She heard an oath from below. Beck's voice had been soft, but still audible above the pulse throbbing inside her head. And then he took the stairs three at a time, reaching Lucy before she'd accomplished even two more steps.

"Don't say a word," he muttered when he lifted her straight off her feet and carried her up the remaining few steps. Before she even had a chance to draw breath, he'd lowered her back down again on the landing, right next to Shelby, who was watching them with astonishment.

Then he strode down the hallway and disappeared

through a doorway. The slam of the door afterward made both her and Shelby jump.

Lucy couldn't shake off the unsteadiness inside her, but she didn't have to let Shelby know how much her father unsettled her. She squeezed the little girl's hand. "Where's your room?"

A shy smile grew on Shelby's face and she started off in the opposite direction that her dad had taken. Lucy followed along. But she couldn't help glancing back along the hallway one more time.

Beck's door remained shut.

Chapter Five

Entering Shelby's bedroom was like entering a fantasy world for a little girl.

The furniture—from the canopy bed that was tucked into a sweet alcove just made for daydreaming, to the built-in bookshelves and cabinets lining two walls—was painted a cheerful, glossy white. The two wide windows that covered half of the third wall had deep, cushioned window seats and airy blue-and-white curtains that matched the cloud of pillows and comforter covering the bed.

Lucy knew that Beck had designed and built the beautiful house because Sarah had mentioned it. But she wondered if he'd also decorated the room himself.

If he had, he'd done a magnificent job.

If he'd hired someone, they'd done a magnificent job.

Either way, the man deserved a lot of credit for giving his daughter a wonderful space of her own.

Shelby pulled her straight to the desk built into the center of the shelves, which were loaded down with every item straight out of a little girl's dreams. Toys. Games. Stuffed animals. And lots and lots of framed photographs, nearly all of which featured a woman with thick, curling auburn hair and pale brown eyes, the same shade as Shelby's.

As the girl dragged the shining white chair away from the desk and pushed aside Gertrude the rabbit to shuffle through a messy stack of oversized papers, Lucy picked up one of the photos. "Is this your mother, Shelby?"

She barely glanced up from her papers. "Uh-huh. Her name was Harmony. That's my middle name, too." She held up one of her drawings. "See?"

Lucy replaced the frame on the shelf above the desk and took the drawing. Even as childishly drawn as it was, she could immediately tell the two figures—one tall with yellow hair, one small with brown—were ballerinas complete with stiff pink tutus. And judging by the glance she got of the other papers, it was a consistent theme. "Very nice." She perched on the side of the canopy bed. "Can I take it home and pin it on my refrigerator?"

The golden-brown eyes widened. She nodded. "Grampa puts my pictures on our 'frigerator, too."

"I'll bet he does." Lucy glanced over the shelves again. As far as she could tell, the only thing missing from the A-Z collection *was* a tutu. "Tell me what kind of things you usually do at day camp."

Shelby swiveled her legs around on the chair and hung her arm over the back. "We play tetherball and hopscotch and run races. And sometimes we go on a field trip. Like to Braden for the swimming pool. And we watch a movie sometimes. They're just baby movies, though. Not like when I go to real school. We'll have big-kid movies then, I bet."

Lucy held back a grin. "Real" school, in Shelby's vernacular, obviously meant first grade. "It sounds like a lot of fun."

Shelby nodded, then her expression fell a little.

Lucy didn't need to turn around to know that Beck had returned. She could feel the pinprick of nerves tingling at the back of her neck.

"Okay, peanut," he said. "You've shown your pictures to Ms. Buchanan and she's probably got other things she wants to do today."

Shelby's chin ducked a little and Lucy wanted badly to point out that she'd been with Shelby for only a few minutes. But she also knew that arguing with Beck in front of his tender daughter wasn't likely to endear her any.

So she pushed off the side of the bed. The rest of the summer stretched out in front of her and she had nothing but time on her hands. And one way or another, she hoped to see the child again. If only to give her a few of her old tutus that were stuffed in storage boxes in her bedroom.

"I'm going to go right home and hang this up," she told Shelby as she held up the drawing. "Thank you so much for letting me have it."

Shelby smiled but it was nowhere near as bright as it had been.

And despite the gaze she could feel coming from behind her, Lucy leaned down and kissed Shelby on the forehead. "I love it," she whispered, "because I think it looks just like you and me."

Then she gave the little girl a wink and mentally girded herself to turn toward Beck.

His expression was just as unsmiling as she'd expected. So naturally, she had to smile even more brightly in the face of it as she moved past him into the hallway.

"Wash your hands and brush your hair," she heard Beck

tell Shelby behind her. "We're meeting Grandpa in town for dinner and we're leaving in a few minutes."

Lucy headed toward the stairs, pretty certain he'd added that last bit more for her benefit than his daughter's. Even though it hurt like hell, she quickly descended. The last thing she wanted to do was prompt another display of his irritated—and unwelcome—chivalry.

When she reached the foot of the stairs, he was already close behind her. The containers she'd brought were sitting on the foyer table and she wondered if the brownies would hit the trash the second she was out of sight. "Did you have a nice weekend with your son?"

"Yes." He moved past her and pulled open the door.

Here's your hat, what's your hurry?

She deliberately dawdled. "He fly out of Cheyenne?"

"Yes."

This was about as productive as conversing with a rock. "Are you working on the addition tomorrow?" she asked doggedly.

His wide shoulders lifted in a sigh. He shifted and his big body seemed to nudge her an inch closer to the doorway even though he didn't touch her at all. "Yes."

"If you bring Shelby, I'd like to give her—"

"No."

"Beck, I'm only—"

"It doesn't matter what you're *only*. It's not a good idea."

Her lips tightened. She glanced at the top of the stairs and saw no sign yet of his daughter. "Why not? Is it just me you object to," she asked softly, "or all women?"

A muscle in his jaw worked. His eyes looked pained. "Does it matter?"

"It does when it affects my friendship with Shelby."

His hand suddenly closed around her elbow, nudging her

outside onto that wide, beautiful porch. Then he closed the door behind them and released her like his hand had been burned. "My daughter doesn't need friends like you."

Stung, she turned on him. "What on earth is *that* supposed to mean?"

His teeth came together for a moment. "I don't mean you personally," he said gruffly.

She raised her eyebrow and folded her arms over her chest, the oversized drawing dangling between her fingers. "Felt pretty personal."

"I'm just trying to protect Shelby. She doesn't need people around who aren't going to *stick* around."

Regret shadowed his eyes, and her irritation fizzled. She could recognize a protective father having grown up with one. "Are you sure you don't mean *you* don't need people around who aren't going to stick around?" she asked softly.

He frowned. "I'm protecting my daughter," he said again. "And I'd appreciate it if you'd just stay out of something you know nothing about. Please," he added raggedly when she opened her mouth to refute that.

Feeling something ache inside, Lucy just looked up at him, but then the door swung inward to reveal Shelby clutching Gertrude by a long ear, and she swallowed whatever it was that churned inside her. "I know more than you think," she managed huskily, and directed another reassuring smile at Shelby, whose gaze was bouncing warily between Lucy and Beck. "Enjoy your dinner," she said before heading down the shallow steps toward her truck.

"See you later, Lucy," Shelby called after her.

She kept her smile in place as she waved again.

But the minute she was in her truck and driving back down that beautifully landscaped drive, her smile died.

Beckett Ventura could claim that he was protecting his

daughter. But she knew with every fiber in her soul that he was protecting himself even more.

She could even understand why.

Lucy was as certain of his attraction to her as she was of her own to him. But the man was clearly still in love with his wife.

Lucy couldn't fight that.

She wasn't sure she'd even want to. No woman could compete with a ghost.

But when it came to Shelby?

Beck didn't know as much as he thought he did about the needs of a motherless daughter.

She hit a rut in the road and the steering wheel jerked under her hands.

She automatically tightened her grip and hit the brakes and when she did so, a killing pain shot through her knee.

She gasped and stared hard at the road ahead of her, not daring to shift her foot until the pain subsided.

She'd been sitting on the side of the road for a full five minutes by the time that happened. A treacherous five minutes during which she had to remind herself that one more pain didn't necessarily mean her knee was worsening instead of improving.

But when she finally, gingerly, pressed the gas pedal, she finished the drive home much more cautiously.

When she arrived, she parked closer to the door than usual and carried Shelby's picture inside where she pinned it right in the center of the wide refrigerator door.

Then she pull out a gelled ice pack and because moving to one of the kitchen chairs was just too much work, she sat down right there on the warm hardwood floor, with her back to the cupboards and pressed the pack over the ache in her knee.

The cold easily penetrated through her jeans and she exhaled with relief, leaning her head wearily back against the cabinet. She studied Shelby's drawing across from her.

Beck needed to understand that no matter how hard he tried or how much he wanted to, as a father he couldn't replace his daughter's need for a woman's attention.

Lucy might not be able to get her knee healed no matter how hard *she* tried, but getting Beck to realize that particular truth about his daughter was one thing she could accomplish. And once she did, she'd be able to know that at least one good thing—a very good thing—resulted from her stupid fall down those stairs.

She was walking with crutches.

Beck watched Lucy maneuver herself out of her truck she'd parked on the side of the ranch house and tuck the metal devices under her arms before swinging herself in his direction.

He grimaced and focused on the exterior sheathing he was putting up before he shot a damn nail through his own thumb.

He really didn't want another encounter with an annoyed and emotional female. Not when he'd already tangled with a six-year-old one that morning.

Day camp had been cancelled again. And when Beck had flatly refused Shelby's begging to come with him to the Lazy-B while he worked, she'd let him know in no uncertain terms that she wasn't happy about the decision.

His painfully shy, quiet little girl had pitched one very large, very loud fit.

Even now, a hot, half day later since he'd left her sulking in the care of her grandfather, Beck still felt stunned. And stung.

And judging by the intent way Lucy was heading toward

him and the way her jaw was determined and set, he figured he was in for more of the same.

So when she finally limped to a stop and faced him, he went on the offensive. "Maybe you've learned the price for overdoing it now that you're stuck on crutches."

Her soft lips tightened. She tucked her crutches to one side and with more grace than someone with an injured knee should have, perched on the top of an unused sawhorse. Only then did he notice the edge of a brace around her knee showing below the hem of her bright pink sundress.

As if she'd noticed him noticing, she twitched her skirt and the brace disappeared from view. "I want to talk to you about Shelby."

So much for the offensive.

"I don't." If he hadn't already decided that he needed to get the addition finished as soon as possible so he wouldn't have any reason or need to spend time at the Lazy-B—more specifically in the vicinity of Lucy Buchanan—he'd have packed up his tools and left.

July or not, he didn't welcome the woman's temporary interest in his daughter any more than he welcomed his reaction to her whenever she came within ten yards of him.

He turned away and slid another board of sheathing off the pile.

"Just because you want to crawl into a grave doesn't mean your daughter deserves having to join you there."

The sheathing fell back on the stack with a crash.

He rounded on her. "How many daughters have *you* raised?"

"None. But I—"

"How many husbands have you buried?"

Her gaze flickered. "None."

"Then until you have, I don't really need your advice, do I?"

"Yes, you do need my advice," she countered, pushing to her feet much more awkwardly than she'd sat. "Or at least some insight into something *you* don't know what it's like to experience." She stared up into his face. "Or did you grow up without a mother, too?"

His jaw went so tight that it felt locked together.

His mother was quite alive and living in Florida where she'd moved after divorcing Stan when Beck was eighteen.

They all exchanged cards and gifts for birthdays and Christmases and that was about the extent of their relationship nowadays. As far as Mary no-longer Ventura was concerned, she'd already put in more than her share of time as wife and mother. And if Beck were fair, he knew that her life hadn't exactly been easy. Not with the way Stan had been drinking back then.

None of which had anything to do with anything. Particularly the woman standing in front of him. "As if you do? I've met *your* parents."

She gave him a pitying look that set his nerves even more on edge. "Belle is my mother in every sense of the word that matters to me." Her voice was quiet. "But she didn't *become* that until I was a teenager."

Dammit to hell.

He turned away and set down his nailer on the stack of sheathing. "I'm sorry. I didn't know that." He blew out a long breath and stared out at the stretch of land beyond the rear yard. Heat waves rose into the air and sweat dripped down his spine. "I hate July," he muttered to himself, then turned around to face her.

The tight smile had died, but what was in her eyes was

worse. It wasn't pity. Nor was it sympathy. It was a look that said she understood what he was feeling.

It was the kind of look he'd seen time and time again on his wife's face.

Only he didn't want understanding. He didn't want empathy. Not from anyone.

He just wanted—needed—to be left alone.

To crawl back into his own grave, even if it was an emotional one, where nothing hurt anymore. But this slip of a woman kept getting in his way.

And it irritated the life out of him.

She had her own things to deal with, like her knee. Why couldn't she just stick to that? "For God's sake, sit down." All of his irritation came out in his tone.

She lifted her eyebrows again. "Because you have such a nice way of asking?"

"Because it seems like you're too stubborn for your own good to take care of yourself the way you should," he countered, and moved past her to grab the crutches she'd left leaning against the sawhorse. His wife had done the same thing. Only her suffering had been where he couldn't see it until it was too late to do anything to help. "Here." He shoved the crutches at her.

She grimaced a little, but took them and tucked them under her arms. It took the weight off her braced leg, although she didn't make any attempt to move away and sit somewhere.

Definitely stubborn.

And irritating.

He shoveled back his hair. "Did she die?"

She didn't have to ask who he meant and shook her head, not seeming shocked by his bluntness. "No. My mother—my natural mother, that is—is alive and well and living in Europe last I heard. I know a death is the worst thing that could possibly happen, but in some ways it might have been easier to deal with if she had died. Being left by choice has its own set of baggage, particularly to a child."

"How old were you?"

"She left right after I was born." She tugged at her ear, looking uncomfortable. "She was a dancer." Then she looked over her shoulder at the house. "Could we just… go inside and talk? It's hot out here. I'll get you something cool to drink."

He wanted to curse all over again. "You shouldn't be getting anyone anything." But she was right. It was a swelteringly hot day. He could take it.

But he, physically at least, was healthy as a horse.

On the other hand, she looked like she was wilting.

He still didn't welcome her interference where Shelby was concerned, but after an unusually long absence, his wife's voice was suddenly back inside his head, chiding him. "Fine. We'll go inside."

Lucy looked relieved and swung her crutches around.

"Wait. We don't have to go around to the front." Even though he knew the dangers, he stopped her with a hand on her shoulder and heat that had nothing to do with the outside temperature streaked up his arm.

She paused and he saw the awareness underneath the questioning glance she sent him.

He dropped his hand and jerked his chin toward the addition beside them. "We can go in through the back." He cleared his throat before she could point out the obvious. That there were no steps yet leading up to the waist-high foundation. "I'll help you up."

"Okay." But she didn't look any happier about it than he was as he lifted her onto the foundation before handing her the crutches again. Because she didn't welcome the attraction, or because she didn't want to need help?

If she were anything like him, probably both.

He jumped up behind her and followed her through the skeletal addition to the rear door of the house. It was still in place though covered with the same heavy plastic sheeting that protected the rest of the house's backside. He pulled out his knife and sliced through the tape holding the barrier at the base and lifted it to one side before pushing the door open for her.

He tried not to notice the warm scent of her as she sidled past him. Once she was through the doorway, he stepped through, too, letting the plastic fall back down behind him.

Coolness immediately enveloped him and he couldn't help but appreciate that at least.

She didn't look at him as she crutched her way across the room to the refrigerator and pulled open the door. "Lemonade or iced tea?"

"Either."

She pulled out a clear pitcher and with a smooth twist, set it on the counter behind her before closing the door again.

He watched her movements as she got down glasses and filled them with lemonade. She obviously didn't need assistance so he didn't offer any. "I fractured a bone in my foot about ten years ago and had to use crutches for a while," he admitted. "I never did get the hang of 'em."

Lucy turned, a wry smile on her face as she held out one of the glasses to him. "Yes, well, I've had lots of practice getting around on the things." She took her own glass and leaving the crutches leaning against the counter, limped her way to the table to sit down. Then she lifted her braced leg onto a chair and her skirt fell away again, revealing the complicated-looking brace that surrounded her leg from high on her calf upward, obviously continuing up her thigh beneath the dress.

He realized he was staring at the perfect curve of her calf below the hinged contraption. He took the chair opposite her, keeping the whole width of the table between them.

Where he couldn't see her leg.

And where he couldn't smell the tantalizing warmth of her so damn easily.

Only then he ended up studying her face.

She had the faintest sprinkling of freckles on her nose, he realized. Pale. Like gold dust.

It matched the ones on her shoulders.

And he wondered then if she had that dusting anywhere else.

He lifted the lemonade and chugged half of it. He needed to get a grip or he'd drive himself into a heart attack before the summer was out. "How long ago did you sprain it?"

"A month ago." She looked at her leg. "I was in a brace even more restrictive than this one for a while." She grimaced. "I really did think I was done with them."

"Maybe you would have been if you'd taken it easier."

"Knowing that you're right doesn't make it more palatable to hear."

She could have easily been describing him, when it came to hearing her telling him what his daughter needed.

"I've always hated being injured," she went on. "It's just a pain." She rolled her eyes and smiled wryly. "Literally and figuratively."

He almost found himself smiling, too. "Have you hurt yourself often dancing?"

"Occasionally. I've actually been lucky in that regard." She sipped her lemonade, then set the glass down again.

Her slender fingertip absently slid up and down the side where the glass was already condensing. "But when I was twelve, I fell off a horse and nearly destroyed my knee. That's how Belle came into our lives at first. She was my last physical therapist." She smiled ruefully. "After a long line of them, who either got sick of living all the way out here, or got sick of their uncooperative patient."

"You, uncooperative?"

She met his gaze, amused. "Hard to believe, I know. Anyway—" she shifted slightly in her seat "—once Belle was in our lives, both my father and I had the good sense to realize what we had. She helped me learn how to walk again—"

He started. *"Walk?"*

She nodded. "Yeah. Until she came I wouldn't even get out of the wheelchair because it was just too hard. I was really lucky, though. I'd had excellent surgeons who put things back together after Humpty fell off the horse. And a father who pretty much rearranged his life to accommodate me, and then, Belle. It took the better part of a year, but together we all succeeded." She shrugged and patted her hand against the complicated looking brace. "I walked. And then I danced." Her lips compressed. "Until now," she added softly.

All because she'd walked in on the slimeball who'd cheated on her, he thought. "Are you really going to be able to dance again?"

Her dark lashes swept down. "One way or the other."

Which meant what? He didn't want to wonder.

He wondered anyway.

She moistened her lips and looked up at him again. "Shelby's lonely," she said bluntly.

Chat time was obviously over. He tried but couldn't

stem the defensiveness rumbling through his veins. "She has friends."

"Not the kind she's lonely for," she said gently.

He shoved out of the chair, needing more space than the kitchen could possibly provide.

What was preferable? Looking at Lucy and wanting things he hadn't wanted in a very long time, or having her point out to him all the reasons why he wasn't a good enough father? "What do you expect me to do? Go out and find myself a wife I don't want just to give her a mother?"

She looked pained. "Of course not. But how many adult women *are* in Shelby's life?"

He opened his mouth to reply, only to stop. "Annie Pope's mother," he finally said but felt his neck itch because he knew good and well that Lisa Pope worked the night shift at the hospital as a nurse. It was Jay Pope who watched their daughter Annie and Shelby on those rare occasions when she spent the night or occasionally played there after school. "Her kindergarten teacher," he added doggedly. "Ms. Crowder."

"Dee Crowder. I know her. I'll bet Shelby wanted to spend extra time at school."

"She likes school," he defended.

"I know. Shelby told me." Her gaze remained steady on his. "It's not unnatural for her to want to latch on to a woman who shows her some attention. Including me."

"It's just because you're a dancer," he countered. "A ballerina. That's the fascination."

"Part of it," she allowed. "And look. I know I'm no child psychologist. I *am* just a dancer." She pressed her hand over her chest and leaned toward him. "But I can tell you, Beck, I do know what she's feeling inside. And it's something I'd like to help with. And—" she lifted her hand before he could open his mouth "—I know you don't want my help for anything. But you're a good dad. You love your daughter and you surely must know that there are some things that even the greatest father can't provide for a daughter. It doesn't mean she loves you any less."

He crossed his arms over the hollowness in his chest. "You're only here for the summer because of that." He jerked his chin toward her propped-up leg. "Are you just bored or what?"

"Is it too hard to believe that I *like* your daughter?"

It wasn't hard to believe.

Just hard to take.

"Everyone likes Shelby. Aside from the mother of a tantrum she threw this morning, she's too sweet for her own good."

"Tantrum?"

"It doesn't matter." He wearily scrubbed his hand down his face but couldn't wipe away the knowledge that—whether he was comfortable with it or not—Lucy had a point.

Shelby was only six now. And as different in personality as she was from Nick when he'd been that age, at six there weren't a helluva lot of differences—far as Beck could tell—between raising a girl and raising a boy.

But those differences would increase the older she got.

He dropped his hand and looked at Lucy. Even being prepared to see the understanding in her gaze didn't soften the way it slammed into his gut.

"Letting Shelby get attached to you isn't the answer. You're only visiting. Sooner or later, you're going to leave. And where will that leave my daughter?"

She pressed her lips together and nodded. "That's true,

but I'll be here for weeks yet. When does school start again?"

He was feeling more and more like a doomed man. But it was information she could easily get from anyone in town. "Last week of August."

"That's a little over a month away. I'm not due back in New York until September after Labor Day." She moistened her lips, and leaned forward in her chair again, unintentionally giving him pretty much a straight view down her scooped neckline to shimmery white lace cups and the swells of soft, female flesh they encased. "She'll be occupied again, probably even more so because it'll be first grade. *Real* school—her words, not mine."

He dragged his gaze away and wrapped his itching palm around the glass he'd left on the table, just to fill it with something other than the urge to fill them with those curves. "Fine," he agreed abruptly. Just cut to the chase and get the hell out of there. "What do you have in mind exactly?"

A fresh light filled her eyes as if she knew she'd already won. She lowered her foot to the floor and stood up, her fingertips resting steepled on the table top. "I'd like to give her dance lessons."

He didn't know why he hadn't seen that coming.

Maybe because his brain was fogged with lust?

"I'm not asking for money or anything," she added quickly when he didn't immediately respond. "That's not what this is about at all."

"Strangely enough," he said deadpan, "I thought it was."

She looked surprised. Then laughed softly. "There *is* a sense of humor in there."

He grimaced. So she'd figured he was a recluse *and* an

ogre. He didn't know why that bugged him when it never had before. "On occasion."

She was still smiling. "Well, maybe those occasions will come more often." Then she blinked a little and brushed her hands down the sides of her dress before carrying her glass to the sink and emptying it down the drain. "I don't want to interfere with her day camp schedule, of course," she said above the water she turned on to rinse out the glass.

"Then when? And where? There's no dance studio in Weaver."

She shook her head and turned toward him again. "Doesn't need to be. We can do it here. Well, we could do it anywhere, for that matter. It's not like we need a proper dance floor just to learn what the five positions are. *Basics,*" she added, obviously reading his blank look. "The basics of dance. But the Marley floor in the barn will be ideal." Her expressive face became even more animated. "So, maybe mornings before she goes to day camp? Or afternoons. Or, you know. Whatever you think works best. I've got nothing but time after all."

"*Now* it's about what I think?"

She tilted her head, giving him a silent look.

"Mornings," he said. "Which morning?"

"All of them?"

"You're one of those give-an-inch, take-a-mile women, aren't you." It wasn't a question.

Her smile widened. "Is that a yes?"

He exhaled. Dammit. How was he supposed to resist that smile? "Yes. During the week."

She actually bounced off her toes and clapped her hands, only to wince when she landed.

"And that—" he put his own glass in the sink and pointed at her "—is only one of the obvious mistakes staring us in the face. You've already overdone it and ended up in a brace. How are you going to keep from making things even worse for yourself with all this?"

"The brace doesn't prevent me from bending my knee, it just stabilizes it when I do." She gave a little plié as if to prove it. "And there're lots of things I can teach Shelby without me going off and doing grand jetés," she dismissed. "So, we start tomorrow?"

He crossed his arms again over his chest. Doomed didn't even begin to describe what he was.

"Before day camp. Assuming it doesn't get cancelled again. She can either come over when I do or my father can shuttle her back and forth." He didn't figure Stan would mind. And if he did, Beck supposed he could start his own work at the Lazy-B later in the morning, so these *dance* lessons didn't start at the crack of dawn.

She was looking at him as if he'd granted her fondest wish, rather than one of his daughter's. "You're doing a good thing, Beck," she assured softly. "Everything is going to be fine."

He wasn't nearly so convinced. "I hope you're right."

Her eyes were soft. "Nobody can replace Harmony," she said quietly. "Not for you. And not for Shelby. But I really believe this will be good for her." Then she reached out and closed her hands over his folded arms.

He felt the warmth of her touch all the way to the base of his spine.

He started to shift away, but she suddenly moistened her lips, looking away from him as she lowered her hands and moved away to reach for her crutches.

Good for his daughter maybe. But hell on him.

And—catching the sudden flush of color over her high cheekbones—he figured she'd be right there with him.

Chapter Six

"So, how are the newborn ballerina and her handsome daddy doing?"

Lucy tucked her cell phone between her shoulder and ear and kept clapping softly, slowly, keeping time for Shelby and her friend Annie, who were solemnly, diligently standing at the freestanding ballet barre positioned in the middle of the barn, practicing tendus. "I don't know about the daddy, but *she's* multiplying," she told Sarah.

"I warned you," her cousin said knowingly. "Word gets out that you're giving a ballet lesson or two in your barn, and the girls will come. You ought to just retire and open up shop in town."

Lucy stopped clapping for a moment, and held the phone away. "Excellent, girls. Keep going."

Both heads—Shelby's dark and Annie's as pale as straw—turned her way with beaming smiles.

"I'll be right back," she told them. "Keep practicing. That's what nine-tenths of ballet is. Practice."

She kept an eye on the two little girls as she tucked the phone back to her ear and stepped closer to the barn door that was opened wide to both the warm morning air and the sounds of Beck working next to the house.

"Honestly, Sarah, they're so darn cute I can hardly stand it," she admitted. As of today, they'd had eight sessions and Annie had joined them after the first five.

Even though Lucy's entire point had been to spend time specifically with Shelby, she hadn't been able to say no when the girl had shyly asked if her friend could join them. And Lucy wasn't sure who was enjoying themselves more. The girls. Or her.

She looked in the direction of the house, although she couldn't see Beck. Because he'd nearly finished the exterior of the addition a few days ago, he was working on the inside.

And even though he'd agreed about the lessons, he hadn't lightened up in any other way in the week and a half since.

If anything, the man had only seemed to become even more withdrawn and quiet.

"You've got miniature Lucy Buchanans in the making," Sarah was teasing, drawing her attention back from the enigma that was Beck Ventura. "Maybe you've got a whole new career budding. Think of the mark you could possibly make on the future dancing world."

"At least it'd be a mark instead of a smudge, which is pretty much all I've left up to this point," she countered ruefully. The pounding of Beck's hammer stopped, leaving nothing but silence and the soft swish of two little girls' feet sliding rhythmically against a dance floor.

It was a familiar sound to Lucy. And a soothing one even though her pupils were just starting out and trying to master the art of a proper point in their soft little ballet slippers.

"So did you call just to see if Megan can have dance lessons, too, or what?"

Sarah laughed. "If she wants lessons, she hasn't said so. No, Leandra and I were talking earlier and figured it was about time we had an afternoon out at the hole."

The "hole," as Sarah called it was the swimming hole, a small, spring-fed lake located on the Double-C. "Sounds great to me," Lucy immediately agreed. "It's been hot as blazes."

"Exactly. Tomorrow's Saturday so everyone should be free. Make sure you let your brother know. Leandra told me even Tabby would try to make it just to catch up with Caleb. She said it had been ages since she'd hung out with him."

Tabby and Caleb had been thick as thieves in high school. "It's been ages since anyone's hung out with my brother," Lucy returned. "The guy's hardly ever here. But I'll tell him if I see him."

"We're gonna do steaks and corn on the cob on the grill and because we're recruiting people without their permission, we nominated you for desserts. We put J.D. on appetizers. She doesn't know that yet, either."

"Fortunately, I'd rather make a dessert than buy bags of chips, which is what she'll probably do," Lucy said, amused. "So what time are you guys heading over there?"

"Maybe noon or so. A little earlier if we can't keep the kids contained. You know the drill. We'll swim and eat and swim some more and hopefully the kids'll be ready to collapse early and give us folks an easy evening."

Lucy did know the drill because there had been plenty of similar occasions while they'd been growing up. But since most of her summers as an adult had been spent touring, her visits home when it was warm enough to actually swim had been few and far between. "It sounds great," she told Sarah again. "See you then."

She tucked her phone in the back pocket of her cutoffs and rejoined her young dancers-in-training. Soon after, Annie Pope's father came to pick up the girls and drive them into town for day camp.

Long after Shelby had squeezed the heck out of her waist with the hug she'd given Lucy before leaving, she stayed in the barn, silently doing barre work herself.

But even as she put her muscles religiously through an endless repetition of slow, measured pliés and relevés, of tendus and ronds de jambe and développés, her mind was elsewhere.

Namely, in the addition where Beck was working. Her parents had told her that Beck would probably not be finished with the addition until after they returned from their trip in August. But from Lucy's perspective, it looked as if he would be done well before that.

The man had been working like he was possessed and she had a fairly strong suspicion that one of the reasons was because the quicker he finished, the sooner he could stop running into *her*.

She breathed out, forcing herself not to let her aching leg drop as she lowered her ankle from the barre. It was harder than it should have been.

Ordinarily, that particular fact would have made her practice the exercises again. And again. But she'd just gotten out of the brace a few days earlier, and she had no desire to end up needing it yet again. So she stopped before her heart was really ready to stop and returned to the house.

Beck had built the wide, brick-lined steps that led up to the new rear entrance of the house at the beginning of the week and even though she'd intentionally avoided getting in his way since he'd agreed to her plan for Shelby, she used them now to enter through the opened doorway.

It was only neighborly to invite the man and his family out for a summer day, wasn't it?

Except the words dried on her lips when she found him working in the new laundry room.

Shirtless.

Reaching above his head to fasten a large cabinet into place, throwing every muscle in his long torso into sharp relief and making the tool belt—and the waist of his faded jeans—droop lower around his hips.

His drill, or whatever it was, whined loudly in the air. He clearly didn't know that Lucy was standing there.

And thank goodness for it because her jaw was dangerously close to dropping.

She wondered, fancifully, if a person's eyeballs could get hot just from looking at something so…exquisitely perfect.

Then the whining stopped. "If you're gonna insist on standing there," his voice came hollowly from inside the cabinet, "at least help me hold this thing up."

She nearly jumped out of her skin. "I didn't think you knew I was here."

He pulled his head out and gave her a baleful look that didn't entirely disguise the flicker of his gaze down to her bare legs and back again. "I knew." His voice was impossibly dry. "So?"

She quickly moved beside him and raised her hands. "Where do I—"

He grabbed one and pressed it against the base of the cabinet. "I've got a ledger board underneath to hold the weight, but another pair of hands is good." He leaned upward again, reaching high into the cabinet, and the air filled with noise from the power tool again.

If she turned her head three inches, her nose would touch his chest.

She clamped her tongue between her teeth and closed her eyes. Only that really was no help because her mind immediately conjured wholly inappropriate visions of her touching that wide, wide chest.

Her eyes popped open again.

Probably, Beck had the right idea.

Stay as far away from one another as humanly possible.

Forget neighborly invitations. Just do what they needed to do.

In his case, finish her parents' addition. And in hers, spend time with Shelby.

Not Shelby's ridiculously sexy and emotionally unavailable father.

She'd already tried to have a relationship with a man whose heart wasn't on the same page as hers. Did she really want to repeat the exercise?

She realized her gaze was slowly—heaven help her, *lasciviously*—traveling the path made by the sprinkling of soft dark hair on his chest as it narrowed from his pecs to a thin line over his ridged abdomen. All the men she knew in New York would have gotten rid of that hair.

She pressed her lips together and swallowed hard. Fortunately, a moment later, the shrill noise ceased and he moved away, taking the heat with him that had seemed to waft off him and wrap enticingly around her senses.

"You can let go now," he finally said. "Cabinet's secure."

She flushed and lowered her hands. "You're really making a lot of progress in here."

He leaned over to pick up the bottle of water sitting on the floor next to the cabinets yet to be installed and his jeans tightened over his rear. "Should be done in here with the cabs today—" he straightened and turned toward her again "—and then I can move the appliances and gut the old laundry room." He lifted the bottle to his lips and drank thirstily.

She realized she wasn't really listening because she was too busy looking, and quickly averted her eyes. "That's nice," she said quickly and started edging for the doorway. "Do you, um, need more water or anything?"

His gaze was steady on her face and it was a full ten seconds before he shook his head.

It felt like a lifetime.

"Okay." She stepped out of the laundry room and into the spacious open area that would soon be the new family room, and drew in a silent breath. She was a coward, that's what she was.

It was a simple enough invitation to join a group of people that she, personally, really enjoyed even if they *were* her family members. Shelby would have fun because there'd be lots of other kids. And Beck could even bring his father along, if he wanted. The more the merrier after all. It wasn't as if she'd planned to invite him to a private celebration for two.

He was probably going to say no, anyway.

But he'd said yes about Shelby before she'd really expected him to, hadn't he?

The debate inside her head annoyed her to no end and she whirled around to stick her head back in the laundry room, only to pull up short.

He was standing in the doorway watching her. "Something wrong?"

"No." She smiled brightly. Too brightly, she was afraid, but there was nothing she could do about it now. "A bunch of us are getting together tomorrow for a swim and a cookout. I...I wondered if you and your family would like to join us." She moistened her lips, not at all accustomed to the nervousness she felt. "We'll be over at the Double-C. My grandparents live there and it doesn't take long to get there heading through Weaver and—"

"I have heard of it." His voice was bland, but she still felt herself flush a little again. Of course he had. Anyone who lived in the state knew about the Double-C.

"Right." She realized she was picking at the fraying hem of her shorts when his gaze dropped to her legs again. She quickly pushed her fingers into the pockets instead. "I can guarantee cool water to swim in, cold beer and soda to drink and the best steak—Double-C brand, naturally—that you can sink your teeth into. Shelby told me she knows how to swim and—"

"Okay."

Her mouth stayed open even though the words dried up.

"Unless you want to keep on with the pitch," he finally said, sounding vaguely amused. "Do what you've got to do, 'cause I know that's your style anyway. But I do want to get those cabinets done. And, yes, Shelby does swim. Like a fish."

"Right. Okay, then. Um, tomorrow around noon. Do you, um, want me to pick you up on the way?"

"No."

Just that. To the point.

She really didn't know what to think about the man. "Okay, then. When you get to the C, just keep heading east a few miles out from the big house. The hole's surrounded by a huge stand of trees and lilac bushes almost out of nowhere, so it's not hard to miss. The ground's soft enough to sit on, but feel free to bring chairs if you want.

And towels for swimming. Other than that, all you need to bring is yourselves."

He nodded, then swung the giant nail gun he was holding at his side onto his shoulder and turned back into the laundry room.

Feeling shaky inside, she quickly went inside the house. She'd intended to go upstairs and grab a shower. A cold one was what she obviously needed.

Only staying in the house with Beck working on the other side of a few walls made the place feel too claustrophobic. So she grabbed her purse and a set of keys. "Running to town," she yelled as she headed toward the front of the house and the door there. Just in case he was listening.

But as she flew down the road in one of her dad's pickup trucks toward Weaver, she knew that what she really was doing, was running *from*.

Namely the fact that her interest in Beckett Ventura had rapidly—futilely—swelled beyond even the farthest boundaries of what could be considered neighborliness.

"Where's Caleb?" Sarah asked when Lucy got out of the truck she'd parked alongside the half-dozen others already clustered near the swimming hole the next afternoon.

None of the trucks were Beck's, she noticed as she reached back inside to grab the containers sitting on her seat. "I left a message on his cell phone. He, in turn, left a scrawled note on the refrigerator door which I saw this morning, that he'd make it if he could." She turned and handed off some of her load to Sarah. "It's the only evidence that he was home at all since yesterday and he was gone again this morning. I have *no* idea what's keeping him so occupied."

They reached the clearing through the trees where Leandra and J.D. were already setting out food on a folding table. Sarah's two older children, Megan and Eli, were clambering over the boulders along the edge of the water, while her husband, Max, was already in the water with four-year-old Ben on his shoulders. Lucy also spotted J.D.'s twin stepsons, Zach and Connor, looking like wet seals bobbing up and down beneath the water's surface. Their father, Jake, was watching from the bank, holding his and J.D.'s baby, Tucker, and smiling. His aunt Susan was stretched out on a folding lounge next to him, reading a book.

"Where's Evan?" Lucy didn't immediately spot Leandra's husband.

"He got called out on a colicky horse," Leandra said. "He'll try to make it later."

"Any news on Angel yet?"

J.D. shook her head. "I talked to my very impatient sister this morning. She's not real happy that yesterday came and went with no baby. She had her doctor's appointment last week and everything's looking good, though, and they've already told her they won't let her go too long before inducing labor."

"You going to go over and help for a few days?"

"No, she's not," Jake said loudly from bankside.

J.D. just grinned and waved her husband off. "He's afraid I'm going to leave him alone with Tuck and the boys," she whispered. "He *hates* changing diapers. I caught him actually trying to bribe Connor into doing it the other day."

"Sounds like a typical man to me," Tara said, walking up with a stack of paper plates and cups under one arm and her one-year-old, Aidan, under the other. "Axel always manages to somehow disappear whenever there's a diaper change coming."

Lucy grabbed the plates and cups and leaned over to nuzzle her nose against the toddler's. He grinned, showing off his little white teeth and slapped her face. "Can I take him?"

"Please." Tara smiled wryly and Lucy plucked the boy out of her cousin-in-law's arms, swinging him around before hugging him close.

The boy chortled and jabbered away, kicking his legs.

Lucy grinned back. "I have no idea what you're saying, but it's *fascinating*."

"He talks nonstop," Axel drawled, coming up behind them with an enormous ice chest in his arms that he set next to the table. "Don't you, bud?" He stuck his face in front of his son's, who squealed and kicked even harder.

"Daddy, daddy, daaaaaaaaaddy!"

"Now that's pretty understandable," Lucy admitted, handing him over to his dad before he completely jumped out of her arms.

Axel swung Aidan onto his shoulder and the boy's fingers grabbed hold of great hunks of his dad's blond hair. "Looks like most of the gang's all here." He sketched a wave toward Jake and Max. "Ryan and Mall were just driving up. I think I saw Courtney sitting in the back with Chloe even."

"And Casey and Erik went on a beer run," Leandra added, naming two more of their cousins. "They should be back anytime now."

Lucy rubbed her palms down the back of her cutoff jeans. "I, uh, I invited a few more," she admitted and felt several sets of eyes swivel her way.

"More the merrier," Axel commented easily on his way toward the water's edge.

Sarah, however, was looking at her knowingly. "Your friendly neighborhood rancher-slash-builder, perhaps?"

"Yes." She shrugged casually. "All of the Venturas, actually." She nodded toward Susan Reeves across the water.

"That night at Colbys it looked like Stan was pretty taken with Susan. And Shelby will fit right in with all the kids here. She's so shy, but this crowd's not going to let that stand in their way. She'll have a blast."

Sarah nodded, but she clearly wasn't fooled. "You know I agree with Ax. We all do. The more the merrier. But are you sure you're not getting into something…else?"

Lucy wasn't sure of anything and her cousin obviously knew it. "I just want to see them all have a good time," she insisted. "Maybe see a smile on Beck's face."

"Good luck with that," J.D. murmured as she tore open a bag of tortilla chips and pulled out a handful. "Jake met with the guy a while back to see if he'd be interested in designing the horse barns out at our new place and he said he'd never met anyone so solemn."

"Beck's working on Crossing West?" J.D. had met Jake Forrest when she'd worked as a horse trainer for him at Forrest's Crossing, his thoroughbred farm in Georgia. He'd also been president of Forco, one of the largest textile firms in the country. But then he'd followed J.D. back to Wyoming and they'd gotten married, and now Jake's sister had assumed the helm of their family business and he had turned his focus solely to horses. He still raced the thoroughbreds he bred, but now he and J.D. were building Crossing West outside of Weaver where it wouldn't necessarily be thoroughbreds running in the fields but rescue horses.

"Nope." J.D. was succinct. "He turned Jake down. Didn't say why." She rolled her eyes a little and smiled faintly. "But as we all know, not many people ever turn down my husband. It's just made him more determined than ever to get Beck on the project. Jake says he's one of the most well-regarded architects of his generation, but he up and sold his entire practice a few years ago."

Lucy stared. She'd known he was an architect, but she hadn't known that. Given the timing, she assumed he'd left his practice around the time his wife had died. "Well," she spread her hands, "he said he'd come. So…I hope everyone's okay with it."

"Of course," Sarah assured.

"Heck, yeah," J.D. agreed. "My husband's probably going to try to use the situation to his advantage, but maybe I can keep him otherwise occupied." She batted her lashes.

"Take off the shirt covering your swimsuit," Leandra advised drily. "That usually does the trick."

J.D. laughed and did just that, whipping her oversized shirt off her head to reveal the shining aqua one-piece that showed off a figure just as whipcord lean now as it had been before she'd had Tucker nearly five months earlier. She tossed the shirt aside before sauntering toward the water.

And they all laughed outright when Jake's dark head swiveled in his wife's direction like a heat-seeking missile.

"They're still newlyweds," Sarah said.

"You're all still newlyweds as far as I'm concerned," Lucy countered. The longest any of her cousins had been married was three or four years. She looked back through the trees when she heard footsteps crunching over the ground.

But it was just Casey and Erik returning with the beer and her pulse settled back down again. They also had cases of soda with them, and for several minutes after that, Lucy kept herself busy helping them store the bottles and cans inside the coolers.

She was sweating by the time she was through. She spread her own beach towel out on the bumpy ground that was made soft by the clover that grew thick and lush right down to the water's edge, peeled off her T-shirt and toed off her sandals, and headed toward the boulders. Specifically the largest—and flattest—one that stuck out over the water. She grabbed the thick rope that dangled down from the tree branches above and felt the familiar, rough knots against her palms.

Lucy looked from the trees where there was still no sign of Beck, back to the water where her cousins had all gravitated, splashing babies' hands and tossing the older kids around. Before the hollowness inside her could get too deep, she took a bounding leap with the rope in her fists and swung out over the water, dropping through the surface with a splash.

She came up shivering and shoved the hair out of her face. "Oh my *God*," she choked on a laugh. "I forgot how freaking cold it is!"

Beck could hear the laughter and the screams even before he parked his truck next to the haphazard collection of vehicles.

"You're doing the right thing," Stan said, sitting next to him.

Beck grimaced at his father. Spending the anniversary of his wife's death like a hermit hadn't made the day pass any easier the previous year or the year before that. But he seriously doubted that spending the day this year among people he barely knew was going to be any better.

So why on earth had he agreed to come when Lucy had asked?

"Daddy, come *on*." Shelby leaned over the back of his seat as far as her safety belt would allow.

And maybe the fact that she hadn't whispered it was the reason why. She hadn't been whispering for a week now, and the only thing different in their life was her ballet lessons with Lucy.

He was grateful for that. But that didn't mean he was happy about his daughter's fascination with the woman. Lucy was still going to leave, sooner or later, and he didn't want Shelby heartbroken as a result.

And yet, here they were.

He exhaled roughly, shut off the engine and got out. His father did, too, and opened the back door for Shelby while Beck grabbed the towels and the folding lawn chairs they'd picked up on their way through Weaver at the big-box store on the edge of town.

Shelby chased ahead, poor Gertrude flopping by the ear she was clutching, and Beck had to bite back the words cautioning her to slow down. When he reached the clearing just a few seconds after her, the first thing he saw was Lucy.

She was wearing a deep red bikini top and a pair of soaking wet cutoffs that hung so low on her bare hips that he couldn't help but wonder if she was wearing anything else beneath.

She was standing on an enormous, flat rock, clutching the end of a rope fastened above her and even as he watched, she let out a whoop and swung out over the water, her wet hair streaming in the air behind. And then she let go of the rope and sailed, shapely butt first, into the swimming hole. Which—a small portion of his working mind recognized—was more like a lake than a mere "hole."

She came up laughing and slicking her hair back from her face, and when her gaze turned in his direction, the sparkle in those aquamarine blues hit him square in the gut.

"Hey!" Her head bobbed above the water as she stroked toward them until her feet must have been able to reach bottom and she began walking, rising out of the water like some sort of teenage boy's fantasy.

Or a grown man's.

"You *did* come." She was smiling. "I was beginning to wonder if you'd changed your mind. I'm glad you didn't."

The smile felt like it was all for him, but she looked downward toward Shelby and leaned over his daughter, dribbling water on her.

Shelby giggled and squirmed and wrapped her arms around Lucy's middle, hugging her tightly as her face beamed.

"If you're going to get wet hugging me," Lucy told her, "you might as well get wet in the water. You have some catching up to do. We've all been in the water at least an hour."

Shelby's head swiveled toward him. "Can I?"

Beck swallowed his misgivings and nodded. "That's what we came for." It was just as much a reminder to himself as permission for her.

In a flash, Shelby was out of her sundress and sandals and bouncing through the clover in the purple bathing suit she'd had on underneath. Her hand clutched Lucy's as they splashed into the water.

His father's hand closed over his shoulder for a second, squeezing. "This is a good thing," Stan said under his breath. Then he, too, was heading off toward the lake. Not surprisingly, his aim wasn't the water but the attractive Susan Reeves who'd leaned up on one elbow from the lounge where she was laying to watch his approach.

Beck dumped the chairs and the towels on the ground and slowly leaned over to pick up Gertrude, lying discarded along with Shelby's dress.

Everyone was moving on.

Everyone except him.

He looked away from the merriment going on in the water and unfolded the chairs.

"Here." A bottle of beer came at him from the side and he looked up to see Jake Forrest holding it. "You look like you need it."

"Shows, huh?"

Jake smiled faintly. He was holding a beer himself, and he sat down easily in one of Beck's cheap lawn chairs as if he'd been invited. "Changed your mind about that job I proposed?"

Beck bit back a sigh and sat, too. He didn't really want the beer, but he twisted off the top, just for something to focus on. "No."

"I'd think a man like you would get bored playing around with small-time construction jobs like the room you're doing for Cage and Belle."

"You'd be wrong, then." Beck tipped the bottle to his lips and swallowed. "I grew up working as much construction as I did working on a ranch. It was only because of my late—" he made himself say the word "—wife that I got into architecture." His gaze strayed back to Lucy, who was standing on one of the smaller boulders, this time with his soaking-wet daughter shivering beside her. "Is that water deep?"

"Deep enough they won't hurt themselves jumping in," Jake assured. "Why'd you give up architecture?"

Beck eyed the other man. "None of your business," he returned just as evenly.

Jake didn't look fazed. Beck hadn't figured the man would. He might have walked away from a fairly successful career, but he damn sure hadn't ever run a company the likes of Forco, which employed people all over the country.

He sat back in his chair. "My dad's interested in your aunt," he commented just to change the subject.

"She seems interested in him. Is that a problem?" Jake sat forward suddenly. "Zach." His voice was warning and one of the kids in the water guiltily set the frog he'd been holding behind a skinny girl's head down on the bank. Jake sat back again and propped his ankle on his knee. It was obvious that he, too, at some point had been in the water.

"No," Beck returned truthfully. "Not a problem at all."

Jake was silent for a moment. "Would you at least be willing to come out and tour the property?"

Beck's hand tightened around the beer. Before he could find a more or less polite way of declining, a woman's voice interrupted.

"Stop looking so serious over there." Her voice carried over the noise and a second later she slid onto Jake's lap, a smile on her face. Beck recognized her as one of the women who'd been with Lucy at the bar that night. "I'm J.D.," she introduced, sliding an arm around Jake's neck.

"My wife," Jake provided, looking indulgent.

"And you—" J.D. turned to look him in the eye "—are talking business. I can tell."

"So?"

"So," she drawled, "this is a day of fun." Her bright green eyes shifted to Beck. *"Fun,"* she repeated.

"Since when don't you think anything to do with your beloved horses isn't fun?" Jake asked.

"Well, that's true," J.D. allowed with a grin. "But your sons are about ready to drive poor Megan into misery, so maybe you should get back in the water with them."

Jake sighed noisily as he lifted her off his lap and handed her his beer. "Fine." He headed toward the water but glanced at Beck. "We'll talk again."

"Talking won't change my mind," Beck said.

But Jake just smiled faintly as if he knew differently before jumping into the water with a splash that reached all the way back to Beck's feet.

J.D. sat down in the chair that her husband had vacated and tilted the bottle to her lips. "Lucy's not as tough as she appears," she said after a moment.

Beck jerked his gaze away from the woman in question, feeling his jaw tighten. "I beg your pardon?"

J.D. looked at him. "She wasted two years of her life being strung along by a guy who never intended to give her what she deserves."

"I thought she was the principal ballerina." He remembered her telling him that. And that the jerk had replaced her. *And* that she'd defended the guy's actions.

"I'm not talking about dancing."

Beck didn't want to know what Lucy's cousin was talking about. More to the point, he didn't want to face the fact that he knew good and well what J.D. *was* talking about.

"I just don't want to see her getting hurt again," J.D. continued.

"She know you go around putting up warning signs?"

"Nope. And when she finds out now, she's going to want to strangle me." She didn't look unduly worried, though.

"Can't say I blame her," he said mildly.

J.D. smiled but her eyes were still serious. "Everyone always thinks she's the tough New Yorker now, but those of us who know her best know otherwise."

"I knew I shouldn't have come here," he murmured.

"Well, actually," J.D. allowed, "I think the fact that you did is pretty great."

He gave her a look. "Really."

She lifted a hand. "I just wanted to make sure you

know she's got a soft heart. So tread carefully, would you please?"

"I'm not treading anywhere."

"Ah." She stood up and looked at him. "Now that would be a real shame." Leaving the beer sitting on the lawn chair seat, she turned and ran swiftly into the water.

Beck pinched the bridge of his nose and wondered yet again what he'd gotten himself into.

Water droplets fell over his arm and he looked up to see Shelby standing beside him. Her hair was clinging to her face and shoulders and she was shivering. "Ready to be done?" He started to reach for one of the towels he'd brought but she shook her head, looking horrified at the very thought of it.

"Come swim with us," she said instead.

Beck sighed. Maybe the sooner he did, the sooner they could leave. Being around these people was no better for him than being alone would have been. And he had no real desire to let his bad mood affect anyone else. "Okay."

His daughter beamed at him and raced back to the water, jumping in without a second's hesitation.

Possibly because Lucy was standing there waiting, her arms outstretched to catch her.

Go on now. The soft voice whispered inside his head.

Sure. *Now* Harmony's voice made an appearance. He damn near told the voice to take a hike. But he finally rose and pulled off his shirt and with a running start, he cannonballed into the water.

When he came up from the cold depths, his daughter was clapping and Lucy was smiling, looking strangely mischievous. "Ready," he heard her whisper to Shelby.

His daughter nodded. And before he knew what hit him, both wet bodies launched themselves at his shoulders, pushing him back under water.

His arms shot around them both and he kicked to the surface. "That's ganging up," he told Shelby who was giggling wildly. Then he tossed her one-handed into the air. She shrieked and hit the water with a splash.

Which left him only one other wriggling perpetrator caught in his arm and all he could think when he turned his attention on Lucy was that it was a good thing the water was as freezing cold as it was. "This the way you treat all your guests?"

Her legs felt silky as they brushed against his. "Only the really special ones," she assured breathlessly. She pressed her hands against his shoulder and her back arched away from him in her struggle to break free of the arm he had clamped around her waist.

She was a lightweight out of water and the water only made her more so. He lifted her as easily as he had Shelby until she was over his head.

"Don't you dare." Her hands scrabbled at his arms.

He pitched her into the drink.

She came up sputtering, her chin just above the water. "You know, my swimsuit top came off down there."

"Did you find it?" He couldn't see an inch beyond the dark surface of the water.

"Yes."

"Pity." And then, when her eyes widened with surprise, he laughed.

Chapter Seven

Lucy stared. "You're laughing," she said stupidly.

"It has been known to happen." He was still smiling, showing off a dimple in his cheek and a glint in his eyes that just begged to be smiled back at in return.

So she did.

Giddily.

And what if she did look a little goofy, or that she did hover there, treading water, staring and smiling just a little too long into his face?

He'd not only smiled.

He'd laughed.

And she felt as if some miracle had occurred, right before her eyes, and she wasn't even sure how it had come to pass.

"I wanna swing from the rope," Shelby interrupted, swimming over to Lucy and wrapping her arms tightly around her neck. "Can I?"

Lucy kicked a little harder to keep her chin above water.

Shelby felt like a wriggling, wet fish next to her. "That's up to your dad," she told her.

"Please, Daddy, can I?"

Beck looked over to where the rope dangled above the flat boulder. "I don't think so."

"Please?" Shelby reached out with one arm and grabbed his shoulder. Since the girl still had her other hand wrapped in a stranglehold around Lucy, she found herself nearly face-to-face with the man.

He was treading water, too, and their legs brushed again. Long and slow and distractingly.

Almost as if he'd done it deliberately, which he surely wouldn't have.

Would he?

Her breath felt strangled suddenly, and it had nothing whatsoever to do with Shelby's grip.

"I get to jump off the diving board at the swimming pool." Shelby wasn't finished with her case obviously. "And I swim better than even the big kids in swim class. *Please?"*

Lucy could see the softening in his eyes even before his lips twisted. "Fine. But we're going to do it together first." He unlooped her hand from Lucy's neck and his knuckles skimmed along her throat. The nerves in Lucy's chilly skin suddenly went hot and, afraid he'd see, she quickly ducked under the water and swam off, popping back up a few feet away.

But he was already swimming toward the shore with Shelby in tow, and when he gained a foothold, hung his giggling daughter under one arm off his hip and carried her out of the water and over to the boulder.

Lucy watched, rapt, as he set Shelby upright and flipped her around to his back. She crossed her arms around his neck and he took the knotted rope in hand, his gaze clearly judging the sturdiness.

"You're going to fill this hole to overflowing if you don't stop drooling." Sarah swam up beside Lucy, her auburn hair looking like streamers of wet fire around her shoulders.

"I'm not drooling," she dismissed. Pretty much an utter lie.

"Could have fooled me." They watched Beck wrap his hands around the rope just above one of the big knots. "Admit it, Luce," Sarah chided softly. "You're not feeling *neighborly* at all."

Lucy made a face at her cousin but quickly looked back toward the boulder. "He's a good man. And I just think it's nice to see a dad with his daughter," she assured. "He's really quite terrific with her." Then she laughed when Beck gave a leap, Shelby screeched and the pair soared over the water and dropped with a mighty splash.

"So it appears. But you still can't fool me, my dear." Sarah leaned closer. "When's the last time you thought about Lars?"

Lucy's chin dipped under water. She gave Sarah a quick look. "What?"

"Me thinks you're not suffering a broken heart over the jerk, but a longing one for the neighbor instead."

She opened her mouth to deny it, but the words wouldn't come and Sarah gave her a sympathetic look. "Just be careful," she murmured.

"And not fall for a guy who isn't over his wife?" Lucy pasted a grin on her face as Beck and Shelby swam by again toward the shore. Whether it was Shelby who was ready for another go at the rope swing or her father, it was hard to tell. Beck was still smiling and every time Lucy looked at that stretch of mobile lips, something inside her chest tightened. "Don't worry," she told Sarah as she started to follow them out of the hole. "I know how to take care of myself."

But even as she climbed out of the water, her gaze strayed back to Beck. There really *was* no point in worrying over how she felt about Beck.

Because it was already too late.

She'd already started on that long, long fall.

The sun was well below the horizon when the group began to thin. After the food, the boys—Erik and Casey—had departed for finer pastures; namely Colbys where they could play pool and pick up girls. Courtney had left with them because she was on duty at the hospital. Then Leandra and Evan—who had arrived just when they'd started up the fire to cook the steaks and the foil-wrapped corn on the cob—departed with their brood. After them, it was Sarah and Max and their clan who eventually drifted away, also taking J.D. and Jake's twin boys, who were spending the night there with Eli, as well as the tuckered out Tuck, who'd been sound asleep in his carrier for hours.

Judging by the way Jake was hustling J.D. to their vehicle, Lucy knew what *they* would be up to the second they were alone without the kids, and couldn't help grinning to herself when they quickly departed, too.

She leaned back in the low folding beach chair she'd brought along and stretched her toes closer to the fire ring. The flames that had cooked the steaks to charred, juicy perfection had burned low and the wood was mostly glowing hot embers now, but the heat still felt good against the encroaching coolness of the evening. Replete with good food, hours of hot sunshine and cold swimming, she felt in no hurry at all to head back to the Lazy-B.

Of course, that lack of hurry could well have had something to do with Beck because he was still there, too. Along with his daughter, who looked adorable wrapped in her father's miles-too-large T-shirt as she chased around in the clover with Chloe trying to catch fireflies, and his father, who was quite obviously trying to catch something for himself, too—namely Jake's aunt—who hadn't made any effort to depart when her nephew and J.D. had.

Lucy wasn't the only one who noticed either. Mallory, who was sitting beside her in a similar-style chair, leaned close. "I always thought Susan stayed on in Weaver because of Jake and the twins, but watching her now, I'm thinking there was another reason, too."

Lucy smiled faintly and nodded. Her gaze kept straying to Beck, who was sitting across the fire ring from her. He wasn't saying much. Not that she'd really expected him to.

But he was still there…which she hadn't really expected.

The man was a continual surprise.

"Look out. They're on the move," Mallory whispered, sounding amused. Lucy watched Susan begin gathering up her belongings while Stan worked his way around the moonlit swimming hole toward them. She saw him lean down close to Beck, talking softly.

Beck grimaced and she heard him mutter, "Seriously?"

Stan whispered again and in the glow of the firelight she could see Beck's distinctly disgruntled expression. He looked across the fire ring at her. "D'you mind dropping me and Shelby off on your way back home?"

She barely managed to hide her surprise. "Of course not."

He grimaced again at his father, then fumbled in the mess of towels sitting on the ground beside his chair. She saw him hand over his keys to his father.

Within minutes, Stan and Susan were heading through the trees toward the vehicles, hand-in-hand.

"Well, well, well," Ryan murmured once they were gone. "Romance strikes again."

Mallory laughed softly. "I think it's lovely."

So did Lucy. Beck, however, was noticeably silent.

Fortunately, Chloe and Shelby trotted over then before his silence could become awkward. They were full of plans for Shelby to spend the night with Chloe, as long as they could talk their parents into it.

"We'll take her to church with us," Mallory told Beck after agreeing, "and drop her off at your place afterward if it's okay with you?"

With his daughter clinging to one of his arms and Chloe clinging to the other, both passionately pleading for him to allow it, Beck felt as if he was losing all control.

First his father.

Now his daughter.

He wanted to tell the lady doctor no just as badly as he'd wanted to tell his father no.

But Stan was an adult. One with a life to lead, and—as he'd muttered in Beck's ear only minutes earlier—unlike Beck, he was ready to start leading it again.

Shelby, on the other hand, was Beck's young child.

His young child who wasn't whispering to him anymore, and who was clearly coming out of her shell around these people.

He looked across the fire pit.

Lucy was swallowed in a sweater, her long bare legs sticking out from beneath toward the warmth of the fire. Her hair was a bedraggled mess around her face and in the dim light, her eyes looked like pools just as dark as the swimming hole behind them.

He wasn't sure he'd ever wanted a woman more.

"Yeah," he finally said gruffly. "You can go."

The little girls bounced up and down with more energy than any two beings should have after a day of sun and water.

Ryan leaned over toward the fire pit and tossed a toothpick into the flames. "Mebbe we should have had 'em stay at *your* place," he told Beck drily. "It's going to take hours for them to wind down." Then he pushed to his feet and Chloe bounced over to him. He swept her up into his arms, smacked her young cheek with a noisy kiss and tipped her back onto the ground. "You two gather up all your stuff, then, and we'll hit it."

Looking pleased, Lucy got up, too, and moved over to the folding tables that were nearly empty now. She and Mallory finished packing away the leftovers in the few remaining ice chests. The little girls scampered around, giggling and picking up towels and toys. While Mallory and Ryan carried the ice chests to his truck, Beck went over to the tables. "These go, too, I assume?"

"Nope." Lucy turned and propped her backside on one of them. "They can stay. They'll be used again more than once before the summer's out and nobody'll bother them here." She swung her legs a few times and looked away.

"Your knee looks like it's working pretty well again."

She straightened the leg in question and pointed her bare foot. "One step forward, two steps back," she murmured. "But yes. So far so good."

He very nearly wrapped his hand around that slender ankle and sharply arched foot. But just then Ryan and Mallory stepped out of the trees and called to the girls, and he shoved his itching palm into the back pocket of his shorts.

"She's not going to have any clean clothes," he told them, feeling like an idiot for not thinking of it sooner.

Mallory waved that off. "She can wear something of Chloe's. And we have plenty of new toothbrushes on hand." She patted Beck casually on the arm as she passed by him to retrieve her chair. "Don't worry about a thing. We'll take good care of her." She grinned. "I *am* a doctor," she reminded.

Despite himself, Beck smiled a little. He caught up Shelby before she headed through the trees with her new-found friend and gave her a kiss. "Be good."

"I'm always good," she said indignantly. "Dontchyou remember?"

He smoothed his hand over her head. God, he loved this child. "I remember," he assured.

Mollified, she nodded. "Go on now," she said as she headed toward the trees, hand-in-hand with Chloe. "I'll see you tomorrow."

Beck's throat went tight. He nodded and watched his little girl leave. He watched until he heard the start of an engine and the roll of tires. And he watched some more until he heard nothing at all but the soft crackle of the burning wood in the fire pit and the steady chirp of crickets.

"Well." Lucy's voice was soft. "I guess I should smother the firewood."

She was right. Douse the fire. Get the hell out of there and retreat to the safety of their own corners.

But when she slid off the table and started for the fire, his hand seemed to shoot out of its own accord, catching her around her supple upper arm.

His knuckles felt the soft knit of her sweater. And the even softer give of the breast beneath.

"It's not that late yet," he said.

She slowly looked from his hand on her arm up to his face. "No," she agreed after a moment. "It's not. Do you... want to stay?"

He wanted. Period. He pulled his hand away from her arm and shoved both of his hands in his front pockets before he could do something else even more stupid. "Yeah, I want to stay." Which was about the stupidest thing that he could have said.

And he had no desire to retract the words.

Particularly because all he had *was* desire.

Her lashes dipped. "All right, then." She pulled a bottle of water out of her bag and twisted off the cap as she headed toward her chair once more. Her sweater slipped off her bare shoulder as she sat down and stretched her toes toward the fire ring again.

He dragged his eyes away from that curve of taut, smooth skin and went over to his own chair, well away from her.

Only she tsked at that. "This is ridiculous," she muttered and dragged her chair around to his side of the fire. She plopped back down on it. "I'm pretty sure I got rid of my cooties back in the fourth grade."

The grunt of laughter came out of nowhere. "I doubt anyone ever figured you *had* cooties. Even when you were in fourth grade."

She was smiling a little as she lifted the water bottle to her lips.

"I, on the other hand, had 'em big time," he said abruptly. He stared into the fire. "Harmony was the only one who was immune."

"How'd you meet?" Lucy's soft voice seemed to glide over him like a whisper.

"In high school. She's the only girl I ever loved."

"You were lucky." She shifted in her chair and the sweater slipped lower on her arm. "Well, obviously not the way you lost her, but I mean you were lucky to find someone *to* love. Really and truly love."

"Didn't you love the cheating pig?"

She started. "I don't remember using that phrase with you."

"So? Isn't that what he was?"

She shook her head a little and sat back in her chair again. "Yes." Then she sighed faintly. "And I thought I loved him at least. I told myself that someday we'd have more."

"More." He thought about what J.D. had said. "Like marriage?"

"And a family," she admitted. "The normal things that most women want sooner or later, I guess. Even me." She closed her sweater more tightly across her chest. "I was just fooling myself, though. Lars never wanted either one. The whole family and kids thing just isn't his way. Never will be. I should have faced that before. And now...I realize he hurt my pride far more than he hurt anything else."

"And before him?"

She shrugged. "Nobody serious enough to even remember really. I was too busy concentrating on my career." Then she smiled rather impishly. "But *way* before him, I dated Evan for a while."

"Taggart?" He frowned. "Leandra's husband?"

"One and the same. I guess if anyone qualified as my first love—" she lifted her fingers in an air quote "—he'd be it. When I turned thirteen he was at the birthday party that Belle and my dad threw for me. Even though I was a total gimp with my leg torn up the way it was, we danced in the barn." Her grin was quick and mischievous. "My tender heart swooned."

He tried to envision her and the vet together and couldn't. "So what happened?"

"Oh, we grew up, of course. We were friends and we were a habit through most of high school. But I was more interested in dancing than anything else. He was more interested in Leandra, though he didn't have the guts to admit it until it was too late and she'd married his college roommate."

"Ouch."

"It took them a while and plenty of tragedy before they found their way to each other." She picked up a stick and poked it at the embers, sending sparks shooting up into the sky. "They've been married only a handful of years now, but it's hard to imagine either one of them with anyone *but* each other. They're so obviously perfect for one another."

"I figured they'd been married for a long time."

She gave him a look over her temptingly bare shoulder. A small smile played around the corners of her lips. "Why?"

He shrugged, feeling strangely foolish. "I don't know. They...fit."

Her gaze softened. "Yes, they do. Nobody who was here today has been married all that long actually." She looked back at the fire. "Or married at all," she added, obviously referring to herself.

"You're young. You have plenty of time."

She gave a snort of laughter and tossed the stick into the fire. "I'm not young, and you don't need to go around sounding like you're as old as Moses." She pushed to her feet and shrugged out of the sweater, letting it fall onto the seat. "Come on."

He eyed the hand she held out toward him. "Where?"

She tilted her head toward the swimming hole. "Back in the water."

He shook his head. "You're nuts. The water was cold."

"But it'll feel warm now," she assured. "Once you get used to it."

He didn't know why he stood up when he didn't believe her for a second.

The water *had* felt great when it was counteracting the hot sun. But there was no sun now.

Only a fire's ember glow, the moonlight and the occasional glint of a firefly.

She was picking her way to the water's edge, and as she moved, she unfastened her cutoffs. They slipped off and fell to the clover, leaving her in a bikini bottom that was just as brief as the top, and just as maddening to his senses. She stepped out of the denim around her feet and continued to the boulder where the rope hung. But instead of taking the rope to swing over the swimming hole, this time, she just dived off the rock, knifing cleanly, quietly into the water.

Her head bobbed up a moment later. He could see the pale gleam of her wet head and her face. "Come in, Beck," she called softly to him. "The water's fine."

He doubted it, but he was burning from the inside out. So he went over to the same boulder. Did the same dive.

When he came up, she was several feet away.

"The water is not warm," he said emphatically, and saw the gleam of her smile.

"It will be," she promised. "Some things just take a little time. Give it a few minutes. And then you're not going to want to *leave* the water at all." She turned onto her back and the red of her bikini gleamed dark and wet, in stark contrast to her skin that gleamed pale and wet.

And inviting.

He ran his wet hand down his face.

"I used to love coming here at night when I was younger," she mused softly.

"Did you come here with Taggart?"

She flipped over with a little splash and swam past

him. Her smile flashed. "Would you be shocked if I said I did?"

"Shocked?" He shook his head. "Jealous?" He shrugged ruefully. It was quite a step to admit that to himself, much less to her.

She looked more surprised than he felt as she switched directions and swam past him the other way, as nimble as a fish. "As it happens, I did not." Her voice was studiedly casual. "I told you. We were only friends."

"Anyone else, then?"

She laughed softly, much more naturally. "Sadly, no." She rolled onto her back again, floating. The long ends of her hair drifted around her, grazing his chest.

He didn't move away.

"My young heart certainly fantasized a time or two about it," she went on a little dreamily.

His jaw tightened to match the rest of his body. *What were her fantasies now?*

He had to bite back the question but it just circled maddeningly inside his head instead.

"Your dad and Susan seem to be getting pretty close."

"Yeah." He wasn't particularly interested just then in what his father was doing with Susan Reeves. He was, however, intensely interested in the woman floating within arm's reach.

And he couldn't help but feel guilty about that fact.

His head assured him he had no reason to feel guilty. But the weight of the wedding ring he still wore whispered otherwise.

"My wife died three years ago today," he said abruptly. "It took only three months from the day I found her collapsed in our living room until the day cancer stole her for good."

"Beck." She flipped over in the water and swam close

to him. "I'm so sorry." Then she slid her arms around his shoulders and hugged him.

That was *not* the response he'd needed.

"Why didn't you say so before?" Her hands slid over his back, wet. Soothing. And then she let go and water was once more sliding between them.

He damn near pulled her back against him. "I shouldn't have said so now." He wouldn't have if he'd thought it would bring out that full-body contact instead of ensuring she kept her distance. Somebody there needed to have some willpower, and he wasn't certain that it could be him.

"Why not?" She swam in his way when he took a stroke for the shore. "I thought we were becoming…friends."

Then he did reach out. He scooped his arm around her waist and easily pulled her against him again.

Flat against him.

So flat that the hard points of her nipples stabbed him through the fabric of her bathing suit.

So flat that her legs floated up around his, and hugged his hips.

"Is this how it is with all your friends?"

Her lips parted. She stared up at him and wordlessly shook her head.

"Then I'm not sure we're friends," he murmured.

Only the soaking weight of his shorts and her bathing suit separated him from her. And it was the worst sort of temptation to know it. It would take so little to tug both aside. Then there would be nothing at all between them.

Not even the warm, silky water.

Because he'd be somewhere even warmer. Even silkier.

His hands drifted downward where the edge of her bikini hugged the swell of her shapely rear.

Her eyes went heavy and her lips parted softly. Her legs

tightened around his hips, pulling him tighter against her. He could feel the shape of her breasts against his chest so clearly that her swimsuit might never have existed.

"Then what are we?" Her husky whisper tickled his lips.

His fingers flexed against her supple skin. They could be lovers if he wanted. He knew it.

But then what?

Even though it was the last thing he wanted to do, he forced himself to release her. To let go of her warm, wet body and the invitation that was there.

He was going to take nothing. Not on *that* day.

Not from her. Because she deserved more than he'd ever be able—or ready—to give.

"We're better off if we leave it at…neighbors." Even as he said it, he wasn't buying it. "Friendly neighbors," he amended.

This time she didn't try to stop him when he struck out for the shore.

He climbed out of the water and the cool air bit at his skin as he left the warmth of the water behind.

"I think we're more." Her quiet voice carried across the water. "It's okay to admit it if you're afraid, you know." Her voice was gentle, but her gaze felt impossibly intense despite the distance he was putting between them. "Maybe I'm afraid, too."

He looked back at her as he grabbed up a towel. "People often acquire a fear for good reason."

"There's nothing to fear from me," she assured.

He almost laughed. Except there was nothing funny about any of this. "You turn me on," he said huskily and watched her eyes darken and her lips part.

And realizing he was damn close to pitching the towel and all good sense and going back to her, he cleared his throat. "But that's all I have to offer," he added. "So unless you're just looking for one more way to pass the time until you go back to New York, we're better off stopping before things get out of hand." Feeling like a bastard right down to his toes, he dragged the towel over his chest and legs.

She was out of the water much faster than he'd expected and she snatched up her own towel, wrapping it fast around her slender body, but not fast enough to keep him from seeing the rigid peaks of her breasts against the shiny red swimsuit or their rapid rise and fall with her breath. "If you wanted to get my goat, good job." Her voice shook. "First off, not once have I ever implied that you or Shelby were just a means to get me through the summer. And second, I'm quite capable of deciding for myself what—and *whom*—I want. And deciding whether the risk of being hurt again is worth the effort."

And judging by her tone, she was obviously rethinking the whole risk and "whom" thing.

Which was what he'd wanted, wasn't it? For her to lose that compassion that was always in her eyes. To put up her own walls between them so there was no chance she'd be susceptible to the desire he was controlling by the thin skin of his teeth.

If she thought she'd been fooling herself where the cheating ex was concerned, she would be doing just the same now where Beck was concerned.

And he liked her too well to add that onto her plate as well, no matter what she thought.

She folded her low chair with a snap and yanked a pair of flip-flops out of her bag and shoved her feet into them.

"Friendly neighbors," she muttered as she snatched up her shorts from the ground where she'd left him. "You betcha." Without looking at him, she carried her gear into the trees, her feet moving fast and the bottom of the towel swaying around her thighs.

He looked up at the stars. Muttered a low oath when there was nothing but silence inside his head.

He grabbed up his own stuff and followed.

The truck engine was running when he reached it and he climbed in beside her. She didn't say a single word to him on the drive. Not even when they reached his dark house.

He knew he should probably apologize. Say something.

He grabbed his stuff and pushed open the door. "Thanks for the ride."

"What are neighbors for?" But her voice was stiff, and the second he shut the door, she drove away.

Beck went up the front porch and wearily sank down on one of the cushioned chairs there.

He stared out on the drive.

The taillights of Lucy's truck grew dimmer and dimmer until they disappeared altogether.

And still he sat there.

"What the hell am I doing, Harmony?"

But yet again, there was no soft voice inside his head giving him an answer.

Along with Stan and Shelby, even the woman who'd been his conscience for most of his life had deserted him that night. It was no wonder he was making such a mess of things.

And after a long while, he finally went inside the dark, empty house.

Alone.

When Lucy arrived home, the last thing she expected was to run into her brother. Particularly her brother in a clinch with a pretty blonde girl who was definitely *not* Kelly Rasmusson.

They looked as shocked as she felt when she entered the living room, though. Even though she was pretty sure the tracks of the tears she'd shed—as much for Beck and the things he'd shared as for herself—were dry, she busied herself with her stuffed bag long enough to quickly wipe her cheeks. Then she approached them, sticking out her hand toward the unfamiliar girl. "I'm Lucy. Caleb's sister."

The girl—well, young woman, really—looked awkward as she shook Lucy's hand. "I'm Melissa."

Caleb, on the other hand, just looked grim. "Lis and I are at school together."

Because Lucy was rapidly realizing that "Lis" was probably the reason why Caleb had been so absent lately, she wasn't overly surprised at the information. Nor was she feeling inclined to lecture her kid brother about the virtues of fidelity where Kelly was concerned.

She was simply too tired.

Or, rather, her heart just didn't have the stamina for another battle. So she just told Melissa it was nice to meet her, and then headed toward the stairs.

"You're limping again," Caleb said after her.

She just nodded and continued up the stairs.

Yes, she was limping. Because she'd twisted her darn knee when she'd been blindly stomping through the trees and away from Beck.

And the way things seemed just then, she was beginning to feel like she'd never get over the limp, any more than Beck would ever get over losing his wife.

Maybe he was right.

Maybe some things weren't worth the risk.

Chapter Eight

Lucy found Gertrude the next morning.

Shelby's stuffed rabbit was tangled inside the towels that she'd shoved into her tote bag.

She pulled out the rabbit and sat on the side of her bed, holding it in her hands. Since she'd met Beck's daughter, she had never seen her without the rabbit within close proximity. Gertrude went everywhere Shelby went.

But not last night.

She chewed the inside of her lip, then reached for the phone. But she didn't call Beck to see if Shelby had started hunting for the rabbit. Instead, she called Ryan and Mallory.

Even though it was early, she knew they'd be up by now and probably getting ready for church.

Mallory—used to getting calls at all hours anyway—answered on the first ring. "Lucy," she greeted, sounding surprised. "What's wrong?"

Nothing that a heart removal wouldn't cure. "Not a thing. I just wanted to see how you and Ryan fared with the girls last night."

"Fine." Mallory still sounded surprised. "They both passed out much earlier than we expected actually. Ryan's just getting them some breakfast now. French toast. With whipped cream," she added with a laugh. "As if that'll help them sit still through church."

"Great. I, um, I was just curious."

"She's a darling girl. How did things go with Beck after we left?"

Lucy felt her face flush and was glad it was only a phone conversation. "Fine," she lied blithely. "We just finished packing up and left ourselves." An even bigger lie.

"Mmm." Mallory didn't sound entirely convinced. "Guess we'll see you later today at dinner?"

Truthfully, Lucy had forgotten all about Sunday dinner. "Yeah." She searched her memory. "At J.D.'s place today, right?"

"Yup. Hopefully I'll get through the meal this time without having to run over to the hospital for a delivery." Mallory laughed again. "Not that I should complain that the new moms in Weaver are keeping me in business. See you later."

"Later," Lucy echoed and hung up.

She wiggled Gertrude's floppy ears. "Don't worry," she told the stuffed rabbit. "Shelby still loves you."

Gertrude just stared up at her with her glassy black-bead eyes and curving, hand-stitched smile.

Lucy left Gertrude on her nightstand and pushed off the bed. Her knee was still protesting a little but not badly enough to make her reach for the brace lying on the chair in the corner. She left her room, noticed that Caleb's bedroom door was open and peeked in on her way downstairs.

Empty. Bed messily made, not giving her any idea whether he'd actually used it the night before or not.

She made herself some coffee, then went back upstairs to get herself ready for church, too.

As she drove away from the house, Gertrude was on the seat beside her. She'd just give the rabbit to Shelby when she saw her at church.

But as she neared the old Victor place, her foot lifted off the pedal and she suddenly turned.

Her heart was raucously thumping inside her chest and her head warned her that she was making a mistake. Pushing too fast into areas that had been clearly posted against trespass. But she couldn't get her foot to lay off the gas, and she couldn't make her hands turn the wheel back around.

And then it was too late anyway, because she was within sight of that glorious house, and Beck himself was in the front yard. Sitting on a riding mower, cutting swaths across the acres of green, green grass and wearing jeans and a white T-shirt and a dark brown cowboy hat. She knew he'd seen her, too, because that hat turned her direction.

Her mouth ran dry and she pulled to a stop. "Okay, Gertrude," she murmured as she grabbed the rabbit. "Wish me luck."

Then she climbed down from the truck and slowly crossed the grass, heading toward him.

He cut the motor when she got there but didn't budge off the seat. The cowboy hat shaded his face too much for her to see his expression, but the set angle of his jaw wasn't exactly inviting.

She held up the stuffed rabbit. "Somehow this made it into my bag yesterday. I didn't notice until this morning."

He reached down and grabbed the toy. "You look like you're dressed for church. Could have given it to Shelby directly."

He was absolutely correct. She was dressed for church. She could have given it right to his daughter. Feeling self-conscious, she twitched the ankle-length skirt of her gauzy white dress. "I know."

"Then why are you here? After last night, I figured you'd wash your hands of me."

It was still early in the morning, but the sun was already bright and she squinted a little, looking up at him. His wrist was hanging over the wheel of the mower, Gertrude dangling from his hand. She pulled her gaze away from the simple, manly grace of that tanned, strong wrist. "Well, either I'm a glutton for dirty hands, or I'm not that easily frightened off. I know that was your intention. Question is, was it just because of the day, or because of something else?"

His lips twisted. She still couldn't see his eyes and wished badly that she could. "It was a tough day for me," he finally said. "I shouldn't have tried spending it with you."

She hesitated, not sure how to take that. "Sometimes tough days are exactly the kind of days you do need to spend with people who care," she said after a moment. "Just because I haven't lost a spouse doesn't mean I don't recognize how painful it's been for you. And honestly, Beck, the last thing I want is to make anything worse. Not for you. Not for anyone. I'm here for the summer. I just…" She lifted her shoulders, wondering if she was the biggest fool on the planet. "I think you're a nice person."

His hat dipped even lower. "You haven't made things worse," he said in a low voice. "And you're nicer than I am." Then he held up the stuffed animal. "Harmony made this for Shelby. Before she was born." He made a faint sound. "Shelby's never gone a night without it."

Her heart squeezed. She'd figured as much, though she

hadn't realized Shelby's mother had made the stuffed rabbit. "It obviously means a lot to her."

"Maybe."

She swallowed and moistened her lips, feeling like she was treading in a minefield. "Just because Shelby forgot it one night, doesn't mean she's forgetting her mother."

"She barely *remembers* Harmony. All she is to Shelby is a face in a bunch of photographs." He looked away and she saw his wide shoulders move in a mammoth-sized sigh.

Her eyes stung. She wanted to cry. For him. For his heart. And for herself because she would never know what it felt like to be loved so much. Not by him.

She cleared her throat, trying to get rid of the lump there. "Well, I guess I'd better leave you to your chores." She had more than a few of her own to take care of back at the Lazy-B because Caleb seemed to be MIA once again. "I, um, I know you regret it, but I am glad you all came out to the C yesterday."

"I don't regret all of it." The corner of his lips tilted a little. "Just the part where I made an ass of myself."

She shook her head, telling herself to turn around and go. There were some things that she couldn't have in this world and Beck's heart was clearly one of them.

"Look, maybe we can start fresh," she suggested instead. She waved her hand. "You know, forget all about yesterday."

She felt his sidelong glance. "You *are* an optimist if you think I'm going to forget some things." But then he shrugged. "But if you can forget…I can try, too."

Unfortunately, she wasn't ever likely *to* forget.

Not the words they'd spoken. Nor his smiles and laughter. And definitely not the fact that he'd wanted her.

Physically, at least.

"All right, then," she managed as if she weren't shaking

inside. "If you want some breakfast after you're finished, come on over."

His hat turned her way again. He tilted it back an inch and then she *could* see the expression in his hazel eyes. "I thought you were going to church."

She shook her head. "I changed my mind." She forced a small smile. "It's not necessarily a hangable offense around here. And breakfast is pretty much the one meal I'm actually competent at cooking." Afraid he'd find some reason to decline, she turned then. "Offer's open if you want. Neighbor," she added casually, and started across the lawn toward her truck.

The engine of his riding mower started up again.

She blew out a thin breath and focused harder on her truck only to look over in surprise when he drove the mower up beside her, cutting diagonally across the absurdly neat rows he'd already mowed.

His hat was still tilted back an inch on his head. "What are you fixing?"

"Um…what do you *like?*"

His jaw canted slightly. She felt his gaze almost like a physical touch. "Good question," he murmured.

Her mouth ran dry all over again and she sternly warned her heart to just settle down. He'd made it plain the night before where they stood on *that* and she'd do well to remember it. But that didn't mean she'd given up on being friendly.

She racked her brains for breakfast items and felt foolish that it was so difficult. She was a grown woman. She wasn't supposed to lose all her ability to think just because an attractive man was looking her way. "Pancakes? Waffles?" She cleared her throat again. "French toast?"

"Surprise me," he said after a moment. Then he smiled again and hit the throttle of the mower.

Her stomach squiggled around. She raised her voice so he'd hear. "You're coming, then?"

His hat—back down where she couldn't see his eyes again—shifted her way. "So it would seem." He turned the mower back in the other direction and moved away.

Lucy wondered how long it would take him to finish the lawn. Wondered, too, if there were even the fixings for any sort of breakfast back at the house and decided it didn't matter. She wasn't going to be caught dead running to town now. Not after she'd already "casually" invited him. With her luck, she'd be found out and wouldn't that be another jewel of embarrassment?

She'd just use what she found, and raid the freezer in the basement if necessary.

And focusing on the practical at least gave her mind something else to do beside chide herself for making yet another mistake.

She drove home quickly, and fairly flew out of the truck and into the house, only to stop short at the sight of Caleb, sprawled on the living room couch. "When did *you* get in?"

"Few minutes ago."

He looked like hell and even though the problem of producing a decent breakfast for Beck still loomed over her, she sidetracked for a moment and headed toward her brother. "What's wrong?"

"I told Melissa we had to stop seeing each other."

"Oh," she murmured faintly and sat down on the coffee table, facing him. She studied his face. "You don't seem happy about it."

"I'm not." His head was resting against the back cushions of the couch and he threw his arm over his eyes. "But it was the right thing to do."

"Because?"

He glowered at her from beneath the arm. "Because of Kelly. Obviously." He grimaced again and lowered his arm over his eyes once more. "This summer has *sucked,*" he muttered.

At one point—before she'd come home and met a certain neighbor—she would have agreed with him. Hands down.

She pleated the gauzy skirt laying over her knees. "Caleb, are you in love with Kelly?"

He didn't answer right away. "I don't know," he finally said, sounding so defeated that she wanted to hug him like he was still a little boy.

"And Melissa?"

His lips tightened. "Yeah."

No hesitation that time at all.

She looked at him. "If Kelly's not the one who makes you happy, why didn't you break up with *her?*"

"How?" His arm lowered again. "We've been together since junior-damn-high practically." He pushed off the couch. "It's comfortable. And I didn't say I don't love her."

"No," she agreed slowly, "what you said was you weren't certain you were *in* love with her. Maybe it's a fine line, but I think there is a difference. And if you really do care about Kelly, she deserves more than someone who sticks with her just out of comfort or habit. Maybe you ought to think about that."

"I'm going out to check the water troughs for the stock and feed the horses," he said in response, and headed out the front door.

Lucy exhaled. "Well, that went well," she said to the empty room. Caleb was only twenty-one and already he was in love with at least one girl. And judging by the expression that had been on his face, it wasn't the passing fancy sort of "in love" that young people often had.

He was seriously in love.

When she'd been twenty-one, the only thing she'd been in love with had been dance.

Shaking her head a little, she went into the kitchen and pulled open the refrigerator door.

She had a few eggs left over from the baking she'd done for yesterday's cookout. Not enough for scrambled or fried eggs, but enough for waffles.

She dragged out the heavy waffle iron and whipped together the batter. She'd wait to cook them, though, until Beck arrived. Then she unearthed bacon in the freezer downstairs and managed to chip off enough to start cooking in a cast iron skillet. She shredded an enormous baking potato to make hash browns. Hoping he liked onions, and she quickly diced a small one, adding that, too.

She wracked her brain to remember the kind of food her dad liked to eat on Sunday mornings, but all she could think of was the enormous cinnamon rolls from Ruby's Café in town that he loved. And she'd already ruled out a trip to town.

She settled for sectioning a few oranges and arranging them in a pretty dish, only to decide then that the dish was *too* pretty and switched to a simple white bowl.

She didn't want Beck thinking she was making a fuss.

Even if she was.

Satisfied that everything was cooking merrily along, she started to race upstairs and change out of her dress only to turn right around when the phone rang in the kitchen. "Hello?"

"We're getting a new baby," J.D.'s voice sounded jubilant.

Lucy grinned. "When did Angel go into labor?"

"A bit before dawn, I guess. Brody just called a few minutes ago, though. Said she's probably got a few hours to go yet. Mom and Dad are driving over now."

"Are you going?"

"Can't, unfortunately. I have a horse coming in sometime today from Idaho. A real trauma case, from what I understand. I don't want her to arrive without being here, so I'll drive over either later this evening or in the morning. So dinner's still on at our place. Bring that sexy neighbor of yours. I'll let you know when the baby comes."

Before Lucy could caution that Beck wouldn't likely want to go, her cousin had rung off.

She realized the bacon was starting to smoke, and hustled back to the stove, flipping the strips before they burned to a crisp.

And then she had to fan out the kitchen from the smoke.

Which left her no time to run upstairs and change out of her dress, or to talk herself down into some semblance of calm because the doorbell was ringing.

Beck had arrived.

Forget calm.

She hastily poured a measure of waffle batter onto the sizzling hot griddle, spilled some down the side and grimaced because the bell rang again. She left the mess and hurried to the door, yanking it open.

And there he was. Cowboy hat, jeans and all.

She wasn't sure which look she preferred. The cowboy hat. Or the tool belt.

Both were rapidly finding their way into her dreams.

"You gonna let me in?" he asked after a moment.

She flushed and stepped out of the way. "Sorry. Mind's elsewhere. My, um, my cousin. Angeline. She went into labor this morning." Thank goodness she had a viable excuse to fall back on rather than admitting that she'd been simply ogling him. "Just got off the phone with J.D. They're sisters, you see. Oh. Well, maybe you noticed Angel that night at Colbys." She turned and led the way back to the kitchen, knowing she was babbling and not seeming able to stop. "She was out to here," she held her hands way out in front of her belly. "And still looked like she could have stepped off a magazine cover."

The bacon was smoking again when they got to the kitchen and she stifled on oath, hurrying to turn the heat down even more. Then the hashbrowns were sizzling dangerously and she quickly flipped them around in the pan, too.

At this rate she certainly wasn't going to be impressing him with her cooking skills.

Beck coughed a little and squinted against the smoke. "Maybe the window," he suggested drily, and moved past her, taking the matter in his own hands as he threw open the one window the room possessed.

She wanted to groan. "I *can* cook without burning everything."

"Okay." His tone was smooth as glass as he sat at the table and lifted one of the juicy orange sections out of the bowl and popped it in his mouth.

She made a face at him. "Skeptic. I can. I bake, too."

He dropped his hat on the table and nodded agreeably, but there was a faint smile hovering around his lips.

"I made those cakes yesterday," she told him. "The gooey ones that I noticed you had your fingers in more than once."

"They were good," he said mildly. "So were those brownies you made. What're you getting so upset about?"

She exhaled and turned back to the bacon only to remember the waffle iron and pry it open, too.

The waffle stuck. On the top. On the bottom.

And instead of the perfectly golden crisp-on-the-outside, tender-on-the-inside results she'd planned on—based on plenty of past experience, too—she had a stuck-on mess of a waffle that was split clean in half.

"Oh, for the love of Pete!" She tossed her hands out, grabbed the cast iron skillet off the stove and dumped it— and its charred remains—in the sink.

So much for the perfect, casually tossed together breakfast.

She gave him a look. "Don't tell me, the oranges are sour, too."

He had the grace not to grin too widely. "Sweet as can be," he assured.

She let out a resigned laugh. "Well, we've still got hash-browns." Because she hadn't managed to burn them yet. "And waffles, once I clean off this mess."

"I'd have been fine with just a waffle," he said, still smiling. "It's one of my favorite things, actually."

"Now I'm pretty sure you're just being nice." She made a face and turned away from that disarming smile to scrape away the ruined waffle. His wife, the maker of homemade Gertrudes, had also probably been a wonder in the kitchen. "Better stop," she warned lightly, thinking just as much of her own pointless thoughts as she was his words. "I'm not entirely used to it."

"Harmony couldn't make waffles to save her soul," he said.

Almost as if he'd been reading her mind.

She glanced at him. Lifted her eyebrows a little as if the matter was only a mild curiosity. "Oh."

"I always made the waffles. Every Saturday morning like clockwork. Otherwise it would've been those frozen things."

She couldn't help smiling at that. "I see. Any...anything else you were in charge of making?"

"Coffee." He lifted his empty mug. "Yours is better than mine, though."

She shot him a surprised look.

He smiled faintly. "I've helped myself a time or two to the pot you always make in the morning when you're over in the barn doing your...stuff."

She figured she ought to be embarrassed on behalf of all womankind for the pleasure that flooded her. "Glad it hasn't been going to waste," she said faintly. Because he was still holding up the mug—the still-empty mug—she flushed all over again and quickly poured him some.

Then she finished picking out the hot waffle bits, greased the iron better and poured another measure of batter in. It didn't ooze out the sides and satisfied, she scooped up the piping-hot hashbrowns. They, at least, had a satisfyingly crispy look, and she set them on the table in front of him. "Hope you don't mind a few onions." She'd already set out the syrup and butter and she grabbed an orange section for herself before turning back to the waffle.

Sticky juice dripped down the front of her white dress.

She exhaled. Okay. There was just nothing graceful about the way the morning was going. She shook her head, finished eating the segment, popped out the waffle—perfect, at *last*—and forked it onto his plate. "Eat up." She went to the sink and wet a clean towel to dab against her bodice. "I'm just going to go change into something that won't matter what mess I make next."

"Lucy."

She glanced up at him.

"Sit down and just relax, would you please?" He split the big waffle in two and dropped half on her plate across from him. "And eat."

"Oh, I never eat waffles anymore."

He gave her a look as if she'd grown a second head. "Then why the hell are you cooking 'em?"

"Because I thought you'd like one. Caleb does," she added quickly.

"You *never* eat waffles."

"Well, not *never.*" She sat down on her chair. "It's just a lot of starch. Lot of calories." Particularly the way he was eating his half. Drenched in butter that was melting across the hot surface and swimming in syrup.

Her mouth watered.

She grabbed another orange segment.

"And being a dancer you don't want the calories," he guessed the obvious.

"Well, right. Every ounce shows, you know? It was bad enough when I pigged out on that spaghetti your dad sent over for me that first night."

He shook his head a little and forked an enormous bite into his mouth. His eyes narrowed in obvious pleasure. "If you ask me," he said once he'd swallowed, "you could use some extra pounds, not just ounces."

"Well," she wasn't sure that was a compliment or not, and reminded herself that she had no business fishing for one from him. "That's not what Lars will say if I go back to New York."

"If?"

"When," she corrected hurriedly. "When I go back."

His gaze skimmed over her face. "Why do you even want to go back and work with him?"

Her lips parted. "Because my job is there." Such as her job would be if she weren't able to pull off a miracle.

"Dance somewhere else."

She propped her elbows on the table and picked another orange section out of the bowl. "If it were only that easy," she said wryly. "I was with NEBT for nearly ten years. And I worked really hard to get there. Starting over now..." She shook her head. "It's not really an option."

"Because of your knee?"

She grimaced. "Or my age." She'd already admitted that particular fact to him. "Take your pick."

"But they're expecting you back. After Labor Day," he prompted.

"Right." Just not expecting her back as a performing member of the company. Which she *wasn't* willing to admit. Not to him. Not to anyone.

Not yet.

She got up to retrieve the next waffle and glanced at him. "Yes?"

He held out his plate.

She smiled faintly and set the steaming-hot waffle in the center of the syrup that was still flooding the plate, then sat back down at the table. She would cook another waffle if he wanted it, otherwise she'd save the batter for Caleb in case he wanted one later.

She poked at a speck of onion with her fork in the portion of hashbrowns that he hadn't dumped on his plate and lifted it to her mouth.

"No potatoes either, I suppose."

She shrugged. "Not very often."

"Missing out on some of life's pleasures."

She couldn't help but give him a look at that. "I think that's very much a case of the pot calling the kettle."

His lips twisted. He spread more butter on the waffle and added syrup. "Maybe."

She bit the inside of her lip. "Aside from the waffle

thing, what was your wife like?" And then she had to hold her breath, afraid she'd stepped too far over the line, particularly when his gaze lifted to hers for a long moment.

"Stubborn," he finally said, looking back down at his plate. He didn't stop eating, which she was grateful to see. "Beautiful."

"I could see that just from looking at Shelby," she said quietly. Plus, she'd seen all the photographs of the woman in Shelby's bedroom that one day. "You obviously met at a young age?"

He swallowed another mammoth-sized bite of waffle and she got up to pour another helping onto the griddle after all. "High school," he said. "She was pregnant with Nick when we graduated. We eloped." Then he looked at her. "Not just because she was pregnant."

"That fact didn't even occur to me."

"Why not?" He eyed her. "It did to everyone else."

"Because you're obviously still in love with her, even now."

He looked at his waffle again. "She's gone."

"I know." She sat down across from him again and clasped hands together in her lap to keep from reaching across to touch him. "I'm sorry."

"I was never unfaithful to her."

Unlike Lars, Beck was not a cheater.

She chewed the inside of her lip. "Do you feel like you're being unfaithful now?"

He set down his fork. "Lucy—"

"I shouldn't have asked that," she said quickly. Wishing that she hadn't because she wasn't sure if his smile would ever come back now.

He just shook his head. "I used to hear her voice in my

head. Like a conscience. Telling me what to do. What was right. But it stopped. And for the record, when I look at you, all I see is you."

Her mouth dried.

"I didn't expect that. And right now—" his hazel eyes collided with hers "—right now, I'm not sure how I feel about that."

"Well." She felt lightheaded. "That's honest at least."

He gave a wry shake of his head. "Honest or freaking insane," he murmured. "Take your pick."

She moistened her lips. "I, um, I'm sure your conscience works fine all on its own," she finally offered into the thickening silence.

His eyes met hers again. "Maybe. When you go back to New York, are you going back to Lars?"

She started, truly surprised. She tucked her hair behind her ear. Even in the beginning, her feelings for Lars had been lukewarm in comparison to what coursed through her just from sitting in the same room with Beck. "No. He hasn't asked me back. And even if he did, the answer would still be no. The only thing I want back is my career." Which was something she needed to keep her focus on. But the reminder was faint and much too easily overlooked in favor of the man sitting across from her.

"Good," he said flatly. "You deserve better."

"I do." She pressed her lips together for a moment knowing that she was sitting across from a man who was definitely "better" if his heart were only available. "You haven't been with anyone since your wife died, have you." It wasn't a question. She was pretty certain of the answer.

His gaze slid across hers. "Is that an invitation?"

Was it? She swallowed and shook her head. "No." Not yet. "It's just that three years is a long time."

He picked up his fork and stabbed it into the waffle again. "Lately, it's started to seem that way."

Dangerous warmth zipped through her. "Was she your first?"

"We've pretty well strayed far away from the ballpark of *neighborly* conversation."

She didn't look away when his gaze captured hers. "I know." And she still wanted to know. "Was she?"

His eyes narrowed a little and her lips actually tingled when his gaze seemed to drop to them for a brief moment. "Was Lars yours?"

Touché. "No."

"Taggart?"

"Evan? Good grief, no. We never even got close to it. We were just friends." She smiled a little. "Maybe kissing friends for a while," she allowed.

"So who was?"

She hesitated. She couldn't very well evade his question if she wanted an answer to her own, even if she figured he would disapprove. "The choreographer for the first dance company I was with in New York. I was nineteen."

"Choreographers are a habit for you. Were you in love with him?"

She shook her head.

"Then why sleep with him? To get ahead?"

She grimaced. "Not at all. He slept with a lot of dancers, quite honestly. I was the only virgin in the company and was tired of it and I thought he was dashing and powerful and he made my heart beat faster. So I joined the crowd."

His eyebrows lifted a little. "Jesus," he muttered. "That's honest."

But he didn't look disgusted, she decided. Not the way he looked when she talked about Lars.

"So…was your wife *your* first?"

He shook his head.

For some reason, she was relieved. "Second?"

Again, he shook his head. "Do you really want a number?" His voice was dry.

"Perhaps not," she allowed. "You, um, you must have been pretty young, though," she hazarded. He'd already admitted to being high school sweethearts with Harmony.

"Yup." He nudged his plate away. The waffle was gone. "Fourteen years old."

She gaped. "Fourteen?"

"I was a hellion. Would probably still be if I hadn't met Harmony."

She could hardly fathom it. When she'd been fourteen, she'd either been dreaming about famous ballerinas or her favorite horse. Or her first kiss. Certainly not about having sex. She took his plate. "Want another?"

"I want you."

Her fingers slipped on the plate, landing in the sticky, dark syrup.

"Isn't that what this morning is really about?" he asked.

She exhaled carefully and set his plate on the counter. Removed the waffle and turned off the waffle iron. "No." She stared hard at the granite countertop. "Yes." She exhaled. "I don't know, Beck."

She heard the scrape of his chair, and then his arms slid around her from behind.

She caught her breath, her eyes closing.

He slid his hand beneath her loose hair, smoothing it over her shoulder. And she nearly dissolved right then and there when his lips touched the back of her neck.

"This help you decide?" His palm was flat against

her abdomen, burning through the thin, gauzy dress, and then it glided upward, his fingers brushing over her aching breasts.

She nearly whimpered and curled her fingers against the granite. "Yes." *No!* "I mean I think you walked away last night and it was probably the smart thing to do."

His hand slid away slowly, so slowly that she wasn't sure it would, and knew if it didn't, she wouldn't have the strength to resist. Then all he did was reach around her, split the waffle in two, and drop half on his plate before returning to the table.

She let out a breathy, humorless laugh. "You're really hell on a woman's ego, you know."

He looked at her. "I'm hard. I'm hungry. You said no, and you've still got waffles," he said gruffly. "What else do you want me to do?"

She flushed and nearly jumped out of her skin when the telephone rang.

She reached out and her sticky fingers grabbed the phone. It clattered noisily when she picked it up. "Lazy-B."

"Hey, there, Luce."

Her father.

For some reason, she felt as if she were nineteen again and had been caught doing something she shouldn't. "Hi, Dad." She searched her brain for a second. "How's Barcelona?"

Beck's chair scraped as he stood. He licked his thumb and stopped next to her, lowering his head until his lips were near her other ear. "Thanks for breakfast," he murmured and the brush of his breath slipped straight down her spine.

Then he reached around her, grabbed the remaining half of the waffle, and walked out of the kitchen.

A moment later, she heard the front door close.

She sank weakly down onto the chair.

"Luce?"

She moistened her lips. "I'm here, Dad." But barely.

Because most of her senses had trailed right out the door after Beck.

Chapter Nine

Two more days.

Beck stared at the addition around him and thought, *two more days*. He'd be finished with everything, including the final touches, and then he wouldn't have to keep traipsing over to the Lazy-B.

Not that the Lazy-B itself was the problem. That, he knew good and well was the dancer in residence.

He exhaled and picked up the crown molding he'd just cut and started up the ladder.

He could get through two more days.

He might be a freaking basket case, but he could do it.

Then another week after that, Shelby would be starting school again. And Lucy...well he wasn't sure what Lucy would be doing after that.

Except for heading back to New York, that was.

She'd been plenty plain about that particular point.

He shot a finish nail through the length of molding and steadily worked his way to the end.

Couldn't happen soon enough for him.

Maybe then he'd start getting some sleep again without waking up every hour from yet another dream about her. It wasn't just that he was dreaming about making love with her either. That he could have endured well enough, he supposed.

It was all the other dreams that were driving him nuts.

He shook the thoughts out of his head and went back down the ladder. Retrieved the next piece of molding and climbed back up the ladder again.

The rhythm ought to have been soothing. It wasn't.

Nothing was soothing these days around the Lazy-B. Only because every time he worked there, his nerves were on end waiting for one more encounter with her.

But since the morning of the waffles, she'd gone out of her way to avoid *him*.

Guess he'd gotten his answer about sleeping together, hadn't he?

Annoyed with himself even more, he checked his watch. He was picking up Shelby himself that afternoon from day camp because his father had gone off somewhere with Susan for the day.

Since the day out at the Double-C, his father and the woman had been pretty much inseparable.

Beck didn't begrudge his father that. Susan was an attractive, available woman. Why shouldn't Stan go after her?

Unfortunately, Beck still had another two hours to go before it was time to retrieve his daughter. And no reason whatsoever to not finish the crown molding before he did.

Of course once he picked up Shelby, he still wouldn't

have a reprieve from Lucy. Because Shelby was constantly talking about her. Either the ballet lessons or the school picnic on the first day of school that Lucy had promised-promised-promised to go to with Shelby, or the pretty pink tutu that Lucy had given her last week. Or else she was twirling around everywhere they went, insisting to anyone who listened that one day, she was going to be on television the same way that Lucy had been, and dance *so* beautifully...

He could thank Ryan and Mallory for that last bit; they'd evidently introduced Shelby to some old videotape of Lucy dancing on some documentary.

And then he'd spent an hour in the middle of the night when he couldn't sleep trying to search it out on the internet. He'd found loads of mentions about her and NEBT dating back several years. He'd also found a picture of the cheating pig.

Frankly, Beck couldn't envision Lucy with the guy at all. He'd been slick and artificial even in a photograph. And Lucy...well, she was one of the most genuine people he'd ever met.

He reloaded his nailer, grabbed another length of the crown that he'd spent much of the morning measuring and cutting, and went back up the ladder yet again.

He couldn't get away from Lucy, no matter what he tried to do. If Shelby wasn't talking about her, *he* was thinking about her.

He exhaled roughly and somehow managed not to slam the crown molding into place so hard that he'd damage the wood.

Where *was* she anyway?

The ranch truck she drove hadn't been parked outside the barn that morning when he'd gotten there. And aside from mentioning before the weekend that she wouldn't be available for Lucy's ballet lesson that morning, she hadn't given him a reason why.

Not that he'd really invited her to share the information, he acknowledged.

Since the waffle episode, they hadn't shared much at all. As if the things they'd said that morning had been *more* than enough to last awhile.

That was fine and dandy with him.

Talking wasn't his strong suit anyway.

Down the ladder again. But instead of grabbing another piece of molding, he restlessly went into the kitchen. The coffeepot was empty. Dry. He'd finished it off earlier and rinsed it out. He refilled his water bottle from the tap and turned back toward his work, but a movement near the front window caught his eye.

Before he had a chance to move, the door was opening, and there she stood.

Her otherworldly eyes seemed startled to see him standing there, but they didn't look away from his.

Not right away.

"Hi." Her voice was faint but audible. Then she seemed to gather herself and continued forward. Her arms were laden with grocery sacks.

He left the water bottle on the counter and met her halfway. "Here." He lifted several of the bags out of her grasp and tried not to notice the spark of heat that rippled up his spine when his fingers grazed hers. "Lot of food. Planning a party?"

"Not exactly. Just getting ready for Mom and Dad to get back tomorrow." She sidled around him into the kitchen and unloaded her bags on the table. "Everyone's going to want to hear about their trip, so I figured I'd better lay in some extra food."

"What time are they due in?"

"Sometime in the afternoon if their plane is on schedule." She brushed up the crisp sleeves of her man-styled white shirt that hung down around the thighs of her skinny black jeans and began unloading her purchases.

He probably wouldn't quite be finished with the addition. Another day, though, would do it, but not if he spent time lollygagging around with his tongue all but hanging out for the neighbor's daughter.

He set the bags he'd taken from her next to the others and watched her move around the kitchen for a long moment. "You're barely limping at all anymore."

She gave him a startled look. "Yeah." She yanked open the refrigerator door and the big picture that Shelby had given her that day that seemed so long ago now fluttered softly. She shoved the gallon of milk she was holding inside and closed the door. "I actually had an appointment this morning with my old orthopedist. He comes up from my uncle's sports clinic in Cheyenne."

"Your uncle has a sports clinic?" How much more about her would be a surprise?

"Huffington," she said. "It's fairly well known."

Good grief. "Your uncle is *Alex Reed?*"

"You've heard of him?"

Anyone who watched professional or collegiate football—and Beck watched 'em all—had heard of him. The man's clinic was the go-to place for sports injuries. "Yeah." *Get back to work.* The order circled inside his head. He grabbed his water bottle. Headed toward the new, arched doorway that led to the addition. "So what'd the orthopedist say?"

She looked at him. "Everything's good to go," she said smoothly. Except the right corner of her lips turned down, ever so slightly.

She was lying.

He leaned against the archway. "So, back to the company, then," he prompted deliberately.

Her gaze skittered away from his as she pulled a bag of grapes out of the sacks and turned back to the refrigerator. "Mmm-hmm."

"What are you going to be doing when you get there?"

He saw the way her shoulders stiffened beneath the white shirt. "What do you mean?"

"Dancing in the corps?" He knew the term only because the chatty Cathy that his daughter had evolved into had shared it with him. The corps de ballet. Comprised of dancers who weren't soloists. The place that all dancers pretty much started out...or so his daughter had said.

Lucy exhaled suddenly and slapped the refrigerator door closed. "No." Her voice was sharp. "Not the corps. Not anything. I won't be dancing again. Not professionally, anyway, but you've already figured that out for yourself, haven't you?"

There were tears in her eyes.

And he knew he was an even bigger heel.

She made a muffled sound and started to rush out of the kitchen, but he caught her arm. "I'm sorry."

Her throat worked. "Why? This is just the way things go for dancers who can't dance." But her voice was hoarse.

He swallowed an oath and pulled her against him, his hand moving to the back of her head. He felt the shuddering breath she drew way down deep in his gut.

Felt, too, somewhere deep the fact that she didn't pull away.

"What'd the orthopedist say?" he asked quietly.

"Exactly what I already knew." Her voice was thick. Choked. "It's healing, but not well enough to ever dance professionally."

"The way things go sometimes stink to high heaven," he murmured.

She laughed brokenly. "You'd know that better than most people."

He sighed and tucked her head beneath his chin again, and he just held her for long minutes until her breathing finally stopped hitching and her shoulders finally stopped shaking. "Have you let NEBT know?" he asked cautiously.

She made a sound. "It doesn't matter." She pulled out of his arms, wiping her cheeks. "I'm sorry I got your shirt wet."

"It's a T-shirt," he dismissed. "And why doesn't it matter?"

He saw the swallow she took work down her long throat. "I knew before I left New York that I probably wouldn't be going back there in a performing capacity."

He eyed her. "That's not what you've been saying."

"Because I was still holding out some hope!" Her voice rose and fell again. "I thought if I could just go back, prove that I still had what it takes…then maybe I could get the board of directors to overrule Lars. He doesn't have the entire say when it comes to the artists—" She broke off, shaking her head. She swiped her eyes again and yanked a paper towel off the roll to wipe her red nose. "It doesn't matter now. The only thing left for me *is* to go back as ballet master. I'll get to rehearse my own replacement," she added in a raw voice. "Happy day."

"Then don't go back."

"It's my job!"

"Get a new one."

"Oh, like you did?" She eyed him. "Maybe I don't want to walk away from a career that I spent a lifetime building. Ballet was my life. It was all I had."

"What's *that* supposed to mean?"

"I gave up everything for it. A chance to meet a man who might actually *want* to marry me. Have children with me." She shook her head. "I don't even have any excuse to be upset about it. I knew what I was doing. I knew the choices I was making. And God knows I should have known Lars better than I did."

"Then stop talking as if you'll never have that chance. You'll meet someone." He was out of his depth. He wished like hell that Harmony's voice would come back inside his head. Tell him what to say to make Lucy see.

But Harmony's voice had been absent since the night he'd pulled Lucy against him in that warm, silky water.

"You'll fall in love," he added doggedly.

Lucy gave him a long look that had shrill alarms sounding somewhere inside his head. But she just shook her head again, threw away the paper towel she'd bunched in her fist and began unloading the rest of the grocery sacks. "Not everybody gets to have what you had with Harmony." Her voice was low. She turned and opened a cupboard, stowing a box of fancy crackers inside it.

"So what's that mean? You don't even look? You get betrayed by a cheating scumbag and you think that's the end of the line?"

She closed her eyes and sighed. "I'm pathetic, but not that pathetic," she muttered.

"You're not pathetic," he said impatiently.

She turned and looked at him again. "Then what am I?" Her eyes were bloodshot. Fierce. "What *do* you see when you're with me, Beck? You don't even have to answer. Because I already know. You see a woman who wants you. But that's all you see because you buried your heart with your wife!"

His chest hurt. "She was my life."

"And ballet was mine." She turned away from him again. Dashed her hand over her cheeks. "Just…go away. I should never have gotten into any of this with you. As you've said, we're not even friends."

Nor were they lovers.

Which made him wonder what in the hell they *were* because he damn sure couldn't get her out from beneath his skin. For that matter, he wasn't even sure how she'd managed to get there in the first place.

"What is it, then?" he pushed. "Pride? You think being this—" he gestured "—ballet master is beneath you?"

"No!" Her hands flew out to her sides and temper entered her eyes. "Good ballet masters are worth their weight in gold!" She exhaled. "I'd have better hours and thanks to my smart agent years ago, the company's contractually obligated where my pay is concerned. It doesn't matter what I think about it anyway. That's the world I know. And that's the job that's waiting."

"Only if you take it," he said again.

"And what else would I do?" She grimaced. "Ballet isn't as profitable as your architecture firm obviously was. I do have to earn a living!"

"So teach," he said abruptly. "You're getting enough practice with Shelby and her little crew of friends that show up here every day."

But again she shook her head. "I can't stay here."

"Why the hell not?"

"Because of *you!*" Her lips clamped together. She looked even more annoyed. More frustrated. And there were tears in her eyes again. "Because of you," she repeated huskily after a tight silence that he couldn't even attempt to fill.

The alarms were going off again. "I opened that door last week. You were the one who decided not to walk through."

"Sex?" She just shook her head. "That's really what you think this is about?"

"What else?"

She gave him a pitying look that had sweat breaking out at the base of his spine.

"You're not in love with me," he denied flatly. "We met...what? Less than five weeks ago."

"How long was it before you knew you loved Harmony?"

His jaw tightened. The answer swirled in his head. One day. "That's different." They'd been kids. They'd grown into adults together. Everything he'd become was because of those years when they'd been figuring out how to be parents, how to be lovers even when they'd wanted to strangle each other.

"Why?" Her chin lifted. Flags of color splotched her high cheekbones. "Because she's your sainted Harmony and nobody can ever hold a candle to her?" Then she pushed past him. "Of course that's why," she muttered as she rushed out of the room.

He heard her footsteps on the staircase. And then the slam of a door.

He rubbed his hand down his face. "Nice work, Ventura," he muttered.

The table was still covered in groceries. He poked through them, finding the stuff that still needed to be put in the fridge and shoved it onto the nearly empty shelves inside.

Then he went up the stairs.

Only one door was closed and he stopped in front of it. Pressed his forehead against the panel and took a long, deep breath.

"Harmony wasn't a saint," he finally said through the door. "If she had been, she would have wanted to fight a little harder to stay with her family instead of refusing any sort of treatment and simply…giving…up." He had to force the words out from between his clenched teeth. "Just because I loved her didn't mean I was blind. It was her way or no way at all and we spent as much time arguing as we did making up."

The door cracked open and Lucy stood there. "I'm sorry." Her voice was husky. "I shouldn't have said that. It was extremely…unkind."

"Mebbe," he allowed after a moment. "But not necessarily uncalled for." He swallowed past the knot in his chest. "It's easier to put someone on a pedestal than it is to face how things really were."

"You don't need to say that. Not for me."

"I need to say it for myself, then." His fingers wrapped hard around the sides of the doorjamb. "Remembering her as she really was…faults and all…has always hurt just too damn much. She could have chosen to fight," he finished roughly. "And I could have chosen to pay more attention to her instead of my business, and maybe I would have seen earlier that she was getting sick. Before it was too late."

"Oh, Beck," she whispered. "That's why you walked away from your company. And why you won't work with Jake and J.D. now on their big project?" She looked up at him. "Why on earth does everything have to be so complicated?" But there wasn't really a question in her soft voice. And he knew she didn't really expect an answer.

He answered anyway. "Sometimes it just is."

Her lips curved upward sadly. "I suppose you're right. It just is."

If his fingers were stronger, they'd be leaving dents in the door frame. "So what are we going to do about it?"

Surprise drifted through her eyes. "Nothing," she murmured. "What is there *to* do? You won't let yourself be over your wife. And I'm too…emotional—" she said the word carefully "—to just have an affair with you. And heaven knows I don't need mercy sex from you."

Trust her to be honest about it. "I'm not sure it'd be mercy for you, but mercy for me," he managed with an attempt at wry humor.

She smiled faintly, but her gaze shied away from him. "Don't try to persuade me. I'm feeling more than a little weak on that score."

"Lucy." Words clogged in his chest. He cleared his throat. "If I could give anyone more, it—"

She held up her hand. "Don't. Please don't." Her voice went uneven. "I just don't have much resistance where you're concerned. And I don't want either one of us to end up with more regrets."

He knew regrets. He'd known them well before, and since Lucy, they'd turned into his constant shadow. "I have to pick up Shelby from day camp soon."

She caught her upper lip in her teeth for a moment. "Just as well."

He couldn't help himself any longer. He slid his hand behind her neck and tilted her head toward his. Pressed his lips slowly to her forehead. "This has got to be the strangest conversation I've ever had," he whispered.

"For two nonfriends, nonlovers?" Her fingers curled into his chest for a moment. "I guess it is strange."

He lifted his head. Looked at her. "I didn't mean it about the friends. Anyone who can call you a friend is a lucky person."

Her lashes fluttered down to her cheeks. "Oh, great. Go all soft on me *now*."

"There's no danger of that."

Color filled her cheeks again but the long, slow look she gave him had his skin feeling on fire. "You should go pick up Shelby before I tell my own good sense to take a flying leap," she advised.

"You still going to do those lessons with her?"

A frown creased her smooth forehead. "How I feel about your daughter has nothing to do with anything but her," she assured. "If you're still willing to bring her in the mornings, I'm still willing, too."

He nodded once. He really hadn't expected otherwise. She was as consistent as the day was long. "I may be back later. I want to get the crown molding finished."

Whether she welcomed the possibility or not, he couldn't tell. And reminding himself that it shouldn't matter to him anyway did no good.

It mattered.

He unlatched his fingers from the door frame and turned to go. "Are you going to be all right?"

Her gaze met his. "I'm a big girl."

That wasn't really an answer, but he let it go only because he couldn't be late picking up Shelby. Still, turning around and leaving her standing there was a helluva lot harder than it should have been.

When he headed back there again later that evening after dinner with Shelby and his dad and Susan, he wasn't sure if it was the urgency to finish the job as quickly as possible that motivated him, or *her.*

Didn't really matter, he realized, when he arrived at the Lazy-B.

Her truck was parked in its usual spot, but the house was dark. Empty. He even went up the stairs to her bedroom. She wasn't there, either.

He glanced around the room. It was still a young girl's room. Pale pink. Ivory. Worn-out looking ballet shoes hanging from a ribbon on the wall. The only thing that looked out of place was the white shirt crumpled on the foot of the quilt-topped bed.

She had about a million relatives around Weaver. She was probably with one of them. Sharing her problems with the people who loved her.

He should have been relieved. He could work in peace. Not have her around disrupting his concentration just by breathing. He didn't have to see the misery in her expression and know there wasn't a damn thing he could do to fix it.

He went downstairs again, flipped on the lights in the addition and set to work. He finished the crown and the chair rail and even added the finish molding around the built-in shelving he'd constructed even though he hadn't planned getting to that yet either.

She still hadn't returned.

He finally packed up his tools in the toolbox that he'd been leaving inside the house since he'd finished closing in the frame. He turned off the lights. Let himself out and locked up again.

The sun had long set and the oppressive heat of the August day had abated. The sky was clear and studded with stars; the kind of stars you couldn't see in Denver where the city lights were too bright.

He headed around the side of the house and realized there was faint music coming from the barn, though he couldn't see any light shining around the closed barn door. He walked over and slid the wide, tall door aside.

The music—some sort of classical stuff that just sounded mournful to him—was louder. But the place was pitch dark. He reached for the light switch that he knew was inside the door and flipped it on.

Light flickered to life.

And there she was. Standing in the center of the space

wearing a long-sleeved black leotard and pink tights, her hair pinned back in a knot behind her head with her hand gripped around the ballet barre.

He stepped farther into the barn. "You're dancing in the dark?"

"Why not?" She didn't look at him. "I know the moves and that way I don't have to see myself in the mirror doing them." She rose on her toes and one leg—the injured one—swept in a graceful arch around her body. She held it there and for a moment, Beck wished he had a camera just to freeze the moment.

Then she made a disgusted sound and she dropped her foot to the ground.

"What?"

"I can't even manage a decent attitude." She pulled a pin out of her hair and it unfurled around her shoulders.

Attitude, he assumed, meant something in ballet jargon. "How long have you been in here?"

"A few hours." Lucy wrapped her hands around the ballet barre, not looking at him. She'd known when he'd arrived at the house, and like a coward had stayed in the barn. "Is that door still open?"

She could feel his silence all the way across the barn and finally looked toward him.

His eyes were narrowed. He obviously knew she wasn't referring to the barn door.

Then he slowly headed for her, crossing right over her Marley floor in his thick-soled work boots. "Why?"

"Does there have to be a reason why?"

"For you? Yeah."

She chewed the inside of her lip. "I called one of my friends at the company. Isabella. She knows all about my knee."

"What did you tell her?"

She looked at him.

"You're going back. Despite everything."

The back of Lucy's throat burned. "If not there, then somewhere else." After what Izzy had told her, the *somewhere else* was pretty much a necessity because there was no way she would return to NEBT now. She shoved her hair behind her shoulders and looked up at him. "So…are you interested or not?"

He was watching her closely, as if he were trying to divine her thoughts. "What happened?"

"Nothing." She moistened her lips and stepped closer to him. He stiffened. But he stayed rooted in place, even when she shifted close enough that she could feel heat radiating from his body. Her hands trembled as she carefully settled her palms against his chest.

A muscle flexed in his jaw and he wrapped his hands around her wrists. "Lucy, talk to me."

She huffed, more shaken by that than she wanted to admit. "Fine. You know the dancer that Lars replaced me with? Natalia? Well, she's pregnant," she said flatly. "And according to Izzy, Lars actually handed out cigars when they announced it."

"If she's pregnant she's not going to be able to dance for long."

"Yeah, well, that doesn't mean I'm in line for my old job." She tugged her wrists out of Beck's hold and moved away from him. "When Natalia took my position with the company, everybody figured I was jealous, but I wasn't." Her lips twisted. "Angry, yes, but not jealous. Not until now."

"Because she's having a baby with Lars."

"God, no." She shook her head. "Because she's having a baby, period. She's barely twenty-five and she's taking the road that I chose not to." She blew out a breath.

"If you want a baby so badly, have one!"

But she didn't want just a baby. She wanted a family. A mom. A dad. Children.

When she'd been with Lars, she'd let herself be put off when she'd broached the subject with him. She'd *wanted* to go on the tours. She'd *wanted* to perform the dances he'd choreographed just for her. Even though a part of her had wanted more, it was the career that had always won out. Because it had always mattered more.

Now, the career was gone. Not even hope remained.

And that family that she wanted more than ever before?

She wanted that only with *Beck*.

She knew it as certainly as she'd known when she was a girl that she'd be a dancer.

Feeling that burn in the back of her throat again, she propped her foot on the shelf that held the boom box and began untying the ribbons of her pointe shoe. "Single parenthood? By choice?" She shook her head. "Oddly enough, I guess I'm more old-fashioned than that." Her voice went husky. "Angeline's husband was with her for every one of the twelve hours that it took to bring their little Sofia into the world. I want *that*." She pulled the shoe off and leaned over to undo the ribbons on the other foot.

But Beck knelt at her feet first. "Were you really on some documentary?" His fingers slid around her ankle, searching out the knot in the ribbon.

Her breath shortened. "I suppose Shelby told you she watched it."

"Mmm." He'd found the knot and worked it free. Then seemed to take an inordinate amount of time unwinding the ribbons and slowly slipping the shoe off her foot. He looked up as he handed it to her. "She was pretty fascinated."

Feeling more self-conscious than ever, she set the shoe

on the shelf. "It was just a small a cable show that Leandra used to work on. *Walk in the Shoes.* A camera crew followed me around for a few weeks. Going to rehearsals. That sort of thing."

"I'd like to see it someday." He straightened. She couldn't help but be aware of how close he stood.

"There's a copy in the house," she said faintly. "I, um, I could get it for you." She started to move around him to get the slip-on sandals she'd worn when she'd walked over to the barn, but he shifted.

Blocked her way.

And her heart slid dangerously into overdrive.

"Changed your mind about walking through that door, now?"

She stared at him. "Have you?"

He slowly shook his head. His hands closed over her shoulders. "I just want to know why, though."

"It's not because I want a baby right now." She forced a smile, trying to lessen the tension. "I'm on the pill, in case you're worried or something."

He just looked at her and she exhaled, feeling exposed right down to the bone. "All right! Maybe I need to do some moving on of my own. Or maybe I've just had a miserable day and would like something pleasant for a change!"

The corner of his lips kicked upward. "I think we could outdo *pleasant.*"

She had no doubt about that either. His thumbs were slipping beneath the neckline of her leotard, sending nerves tightening up and down her spine. "You don't have to worry. It's not like I'm going to expect anything."

"Ah, Lucy." His voice was low. Regretful. "You should expect everything. You deserve to have that. And if I could—"

Her eyes burned and she lifted her hand, covering his mouth. She couldn't bear to hear the rest.

With him there were no illusions to be broken. He didn't love her. She knew that. But that didn't mean he wasn't a good man. A good man who wanted her.

And for tonight, it was going to be enough. Because it had to be. Because she couldn't back away from him one more time.

"The only thing I expect for either one of us is to forget everything but *this*." She stepped closer until her body brushed his.

His hands slid down her shoulders. Around her waist. He lifted her off her feet until her mouth was level with his. "I've been dreaming about *this*," he murmured and slowly grazed his lips over hers. "But where's your brother?"

She actually felt dizzy and tightened her hands around him. Her legs just seemed to naturally find their way around his hips. Helped, no doubt, by the hands he'd slid beneath her derriere.

"Caleb?" She had to focus her thoughts. "He's fishing for a few days with some of our cousins." He'd actually left a note for her. "Why?"

"I don't want to be interrupted." He brushed a kiss against her mouth again and her fingers tunneled through his thick hair. She kissed the hard line of his jaw; felt the tantalizing bristly roughness against her lips.

"There's nobody here but you and me," she whispered near his ear.

His fingers flexed against her rear. "Are we gonna keep talking?"

She tilted her head back until she could see his face. "I hope not," she admitted breathlessly.

The corners of his eyes crinkled a little, and then his mouth was on hers.

Colors exploded in her mind, sending bolts of heat through every vein. Her legs tightened around him.

And then he was walking, heading toward the barn door.

"Too far." Her voice felt raw. "The mats. By the mirror."

His gaze slid over hers, setting off another liquid wave, and then he carried her to the folded tumbling mats. They were stacked neatly against the mirror that lined part of the barn, and were as high as any bed and almost as wide.

He lowered her until her feet hit the ground. Whatever breath she had left was stolen when he pulled his shirt off over his head. Without thinking, her fingers reached out to stroke over that wealth of hard, broad chest. Down the ridges of his abdomen.

He gave a strangled sound and closed his hand over hers, capturing it flat against his stomach for an aching second before setting it away from him. "You go any further and this is going to be over before we've begun."

She started to slide the leotard off her shoulders, but his hands got in the way. "I've dreamed about undressing you," he murmured. As if he had all the patience in the world, he slowly...so slowly...drew the stretchy fabric down her arms.

Her knees felt weak. "What else have you dreamed?"

His eyes were hooded as he watched the wide neckline of her leotard reach her breasts. He tugged again and it slid lower, beneath the rigid points of her achingly tight nipples. "This." His head dipped and his mouth found one crest. Then the other.

She swallowed a moan, closing her hands around his shoulders. "Beck..."

His mouth burned up her throat. Her jaw. His hands pushed the leotard down past her hips. Her thighs. It slipped down to her feet and then he was leaning over her, rolling down her tights.

She closed her eyes, feeling the brush of his hair against her breast. Her belly. She grabbed his bare shoulders before her knees simply gave way.

And then she was wearing nothing at all except the heat that was in his eyes as he looked at her. "I dreamed about this." He slid his hand along her waist. Her hips. Glided even more slowly over her thigh. Then back up again. Over her abdomen. And lower.

She sucked in a breath as he touched her. She reached for his belt buckle and dragged it free. His fingers swirled. Teased. Her head fell weakly forward onto his chest and she fumbled desperately with his fly, unable to unfasten it quickly enough to suit her. "Wait—" she whispered. "Wait—"

"I dreamed about you," he murmured. "Wet. And dancing for me."

Shivers danced down her spine and she pulled away from him long enough to turn in a very slow pirouette. "This kind of dance?" She stepped back to him until her bare breasts were pressed against his chest. "Or this kind?" She slowly raised her good knee, brushing it deliberately along his thigh, then extended her leg until her pointed toes reached above his shoulder.

He made a rough sound, and slid his hand between them, cupping her boldly. "What do you think?" He kissed her calf, his gaze never letting hers escape as he slid one finger inside. Then another.

She gasped, shuddering. And even before she could settle and gain some sense, he was moving again. And then his jeans were gone and he was pulling her down onto the mats, pulling her down onto him, his hands hard and gentle at the same time as he sank to the very heart of her. His teeth bared and he slowly thrust, filling her until there was nothing but an ever-tightening, ever-spiraling pleasure.

Her lips parted, her breath keening, her fingers tangled with his on her hips. Nothing. *Nothing* had ever felt like this.

"Lucy." His fierce gaze was hot on hers. "*This* dance."

As if she'd been waiting only for that, her head fell back and she cried out his name and splintered into a thousand shining points of ecstasy. And she knew that in this dance at least he was right there with her in that same, exquisite light.

Chapter Ten

Eventually, they made it to the house. And only the fact that Lucy didn't know when, or if, Caleb would be coming in, did she make it past the couch and upstairs to her bedroom before dragging Beck down to her again.

And it was much later still when they finally went in search of food.

"Are you going to fix me waffles again?" Wearing only his jeans and a small grin, he leaned against the counter while she tried to make order out of the groceries that were shoved haphazardly inside the refrigerator.

She gave him a look. "Are you going to make it worth my while?"

He reached out and caught the sash of her robe, tugging on it enough to loosen and gape open over her breasts. "Honey, I've already done that. Three times."

Her cheeks were hot but she held his gaze. "Didn't notice you complaining."

He gave a low chuckle that made every nerve in her body

sing. Then he was reaching past her into the refrigerator and pulled out a bunch of grapes. "Here. You can feed them to me one at a time."

She snorted and retied her robe. "In your dreams."

"Think we've established what's in my dreams," he reminded, looking sexy and satisfied and oh-so-wicked.

She plucked the grapes out of his hands and carried them to the sink, rinsing them off under the faucet. "All right, then, Mr. Ventura." She held up the bunch by the thick stem and wiggled them as she edged toward the doorway. "Let's see what you're made of, then."

He caught her from behind, kissed the nape of her neck through her hair and slipped the grapes out of her suddenly lax fingers. He pulled one free and popped it in her mouth. "My dad and Susan are getting married."

She stopped dead in her tracks, quickly swallowing the succulent grape. "You're kidding!"

"They told us at dinner."

"Well, that's wonderful. Isn't it?"

Beck nodded and pressed himself against her.

He'd known she'd be addictive. He just hadn't counted on *how* addictive.

"Where are they going to live?"

"They plan to build a place of their own somewhere around here if they can find a property they like."

She gave him a quick look. "*They* plan to, or will you build it?"

He gave a casual shrug that didn't feel entirely casual. "I told them I'll design it at least."

She smiled slowly. "I think that's wonderful, Beck."

He just grimaced, hoping to hell she wouldn't make a big deal out of the decision.

It wasn't as if he planned to hang out his shingle again.

Or that he'd been thinking—at all—about Jake Forrest's new project…

Wanting to distract her as much as himself, he wrapped his arm around her waist and slid his hand inside the robe, landing on a velvety smooth swell of hip.

"Have they set a wedding date already?" Her voice went a little breathy.

"Not quite, but they want to do it within the next few months. Neither one of them can think of a reason to wait."

She caught his hand before it could get somewhere really interesting and turned in his arms to loop her hands around his neck. "I can tell you on good authority that Weaver has been the home to some very, very lovely weddings. I'm sure your father and Susan's will be one as well. I wish I could be here to see it."

But she wouldn't be. Because after Labor Day, she was returning to New York. To work at the same place her cheating lover still worked.

There was no reason for his mouth to feel sour but it did. And he suddenly felt an urge to make his mark on her; to make certain that she'd know just what she'd left when she went.

He pulled her robe off her shoulders and hauled her up to his mouth, pinning her between him and the wall behind her back. He heard her soft gasp, and felt her mouth open under his demanding kiss.

"Beck—" she whispered unsteadily when the need for oxygen drove him to finally lift his head.

Yes. He wanted to hear his name on her lips. Only his name. And if that made him the son of a bitch he knew he could be, then so be it. He covered her breasts with his hands, felt the stab of her nipples against his palms and dragged his thumbs over them, catching them until they pearled even more tightly, turning a deep rosy red that begged to be tasted.

But he didn't just taste.

He feasted. He feasted and he drove her until she was practically sobbing in his arms, and only then did he shove aside his jeans and plunge into her, taking her right then and there against the kitchen wall.

But if he'd thought she wouldn't meet his sudden demand, he was wrong. Because even as he took, so did she. And in that moment when he knew he was on the precipice of losing complete control, her glowing aquamarine eyes stared hotly into his and she wrapped her lithe, strong body around his. "Yes," she whispered hoarsely. "Don't stop."

He couldn't have even if he'd wanted to.

And he didn't want to.

And then her eyes fluttered, her lips parted and he felt the exquisite ripples inside her begin to grow. And spread. Her fingers tightened on his shoulders until he felt her nails digging in. And still he drove. Until she cried his name out loud, and those ripples became an endless wave, pulling him under an abyss of pleasure so acute that he didn't care if he ever came up again.

And after, when they finally made it up to her tumbled bed and she curled against him and fell immediately into an exhausted sleep, he was left staring up at the ceiling, drained and spent.

And it scared the hell out of him.

Not just because he wasn't sure whose mark had been made on whom.

But because, once again, he was going to be the one left behind.

Chapter Eleven

He was gone when she woke.

Lucy pushed her tumbled hair out of her eyes and rolled over in bed. Even that much movement had some muscles protesting, but it was the good kind of protest. The kind that reminded her well how they'd been earned.

Making love with Beck. Again. And again.

She exhaled luxuriously, the memories so fresh and vivid that she went hot all over again.

She didn't remember his leaving, but she knew that he would have wanted to be home when Shelby woke. *And* he would be back that day to continue finishing the addition.

Suddenly energized, she climbed out of bed and stripped off the sheets. She pulled on her robe and carried them down to the new laundry room, inhaling the scent of fresh paint and new wood as she filled the washing machine. She smoothed her hand over the satiny surface of the cupboards that Beck had installed and smiled to herself. Belle was going to love the addition, but Lucy was always going to remember watching Beck put the whole thing together.

With the washing machine quietly humming, she went into the kitchen. The clock told her she'd slept later than she'd expected. Of course, she'd had good reason.

Smiling even more, she started a pot of coffee so it would be ready when Beck got there with Shelby. It was Friday and his father was busy with his AA meeting in Braden, which meant that Beck would be shuttling Shelby around that day.

She tidied up the kitchen from their middle-of-the-night refrigerator raid, then hurried back upstairs to shower and get dressed. By the time she got back downstairs, the sheets were done in the washer and she transferred them to the dryer and hurried over to the barn to get ready for that morning's dance lesson.

Beck still hadn't arrived. Not even after the last of the cars came and went, dropping off little girls dressed in everything from the traditional black leotards and pink tights to summer shorts and tank tops.

But no Shelby. And no Beck.

Lucy assigned them a simple dance sequence to practice and called his house. He answered on the fourth ring, when she was nearly ready to give up.

"Shelby woke up with a fever," he said in greeting.

"Oh dear. How bad?"

"Few degrees." His voice was short. "I'm taking her to the pediatrician now."

"Good idea. I won't keep you, then. How about if I come over this afternoon?"

"That's not a good idea."

Something in his voice made her stomach tense. "Why not?"

"School starts soon. And you're going back to New York.

She's already upset at the idea of your leaving, just like I feared."

"What's going on? After yesterday—"

"Lucy." He sounded ragged. "I can't do this. Not to any of us."

Her eyes started burning. "Beck—"

"I'm sorry. Right now, I've got to get Shelby into town. The doc is fitting us in between other patients."

"Right." Her fingers tightened around the phone. "We'll, um, we'll talk later."

But she realized she was only talking to the dial tone. He'd already hung up.

She stared out at the house across from the opened barn door and marshaled her emotions. He was just worried about Shelby, she told herself. And maybe freaked out about how quickly things were moving.

They could deal with that.

She wasn't afraid of waiting, if she had to.

Drawing a deep breath, she slipped her phone into the pocket of her loose sweater and turned back to her little dancers. But the second the last child had departed after the lesson with her parents, she went into the house to grab the truck keys where she'd left them on the counter.

She was going to Beck's whether he invited her or not. And if he was still in town with Shelby, then she would wait.

But before she made it out of the house, she heard the creak of the front door.

Relief swept through her, making her knees feel strangely weak. She left the keys where they lay as she moved toward the kitchen doorway. "You decided to come after—"

"Sweetheart!" Belle dumped the shopping bags and purse she was holding on the hall table and hurried forward, her outstretched arms folding around Lucy before that false relief even had a chance to settle. "Oh, honey, it is *so* good to see your face!" Belle pulled back, her dark eyes sparkling. "And I'll admit this now before your father walks in, but I am *so* glad to be home again. The next time we take a vacation, it is *not* going to be longer than two weeks, and that is that!" She cupped Lucy's cheek with her palm and hugged her again. "So, tell me, how is your knee?" Her eyebrows rose. "Caleb informs me that you underplayed the seriousness a bit."

Lucy was so disappointed that it wasn't Beck who'd arrived that she couldn't even summon up irritation for her brother's lack of discretion. "It's fine," she assured shortly. "As fine as it's ever going to get anyway."

Belle's eyes were narrowed, but boots clomped on the steps outside and Lucy's father walked in, loaded down with suitcases. He dumped them on the floor at his feet, then kissed Lucy's forehead and swept her off her feet in a giant hug. "Your mother—" he jerked his head toward Belle once he'd set Lucy back on her feet "—never told me that suitcases *multiply*."

Belle grinned and waved a hand dismissively. "I didn't figure that some facts of life still needed to be explained to you at your age."

Cage swept his arm around his wife's trim waist and hauled her next to him. "Honey, if you haven't learned by now that we've got the most important facts of life all sewed up, particularly after our vacation, then we haven't been doing something right."

Lucy clapped her hands over her ears. "Please, the children are present." Then she pointed. "Anything I can help carry in?"

"Good heavens, no." Belle sidled out of her husband's hold and took Lucy's arm. "Cage will take care of it. *You* and I are going to catch up."

Lucy nearly groaned, but didn't want to give her father any reason to look more suspicious and shrugged instead. "Let's do it in your new addition," she suggested. "By way of the laundry room. It's seriously drool-worthy. Almost enough to make me enjoy doing the darn chore."

Belle smiled, and they headed through the house.

Lucy did get a small reprieve then because Belle simply stopped and stared in awe as she took in all of Beck's amazing work. She touched the cabinets above her fancy washing machine and dryer with reverent fingertips. "I *knew* it would be lovely. I've been to Beck's place, after all, but…" She broke off, shaking her head with wonder. "This is so much more than I expected."

Then she left the laundry room and went into the new family room. She stood in the center of the space, her gaze running from wood flooring to gleaming windows to high ceilings and all of the trimmings in between. "I can't believe he did so much in such a short time." She glanced at Lucy. "He must have been working nonstop over here. Was the noise and mess very much a bother?"

Lucy tried not to flush. "Not at all. And he's been bringing Shelby," she reminded. She'd told her folks about the dancing lessons when they'd spoken on the phone, though not about how much they'd expanded. "She's such a doll."

"She is," Belle agreed. Her discerning gaze had turned from admiring the improvements to her home to the studied casualness on Lucy's face. "Beck's a fine father, but she needs a mother."

Lucy's face felt warm. "A few of her friends have started coming to the morning lessons as well. They, um, they all just left a few minutes before you arrived, actually. We've been working over in the barn."

"I know," Belle admitted. "I've heard all about your

budding little business from Squire and Gloria." Then she tilted her head slightly and pinned Lucy with a no-nonsense look. "Now, about your knee." She nudged Lucy back into the kitchen and pointed at one of the chairs. "Sit."

Lucy grimaced. "I'm not twelve anymore."

"Then stop acting like it. I know Dr. Valenzuela has seen you twice." Belle pointed at the chair again. "Sit."

Lucy sat.

Belle crouched at her foot and rolled up the stretchy knit of Lucy's dance pants until her knee was revealed. Her knowledgeable, nimble fingers gently felt around Lucy's knee, the muscles above and the muscles below. She had Lucy extend and flex and bend and point and it was almost like a step back into time.

Lucy finally caught her mother's hands in hers and squeezed. "This isn't one that you're going to be able to help me fix," she said huskily.

Belle sat back on her heels. Her eyes were dark and Lucy knew that she didn't have to tell her mother any more than that for her to understand all of the ramifications. "I'm sorry, sweetheart. I wish we'd been here for you. That you didn't have to deal with this all on your own."

"I know." Lucy's throat tightened. "But I needed you two to have that trip. You've waited nearly all of your married life for it." She swallowed. "And I haven't been all alone. Caleb—"

"Has been gone more often than not," Belle said tartly. "He admitted as much when we last spoke, but I'd already heard about it from the family before then."

Lucy wondered what else her parents might have heard from "the family." They all could complain that it was just the other residents of the Weaver community who were the biggest gossips, but the fact was nothing much happened among the extensive Clay family without word quickly traveling on the family's own grapevine. Sometimes, it was a curse as much as it was a blessing.

"And Beck's been here," she added casually.

"And?"

"And nothing."

Belle lifted an eyebrow. "Sweetheart, you can either tell me what's *really* going on with you and Beck, or you can tell your dad and me when he comes in here in two minutes."

"You're going to tell him anyway."

"Yes, I am. But it might be easier for him to hear, coming from me first, that his baby girl has fallen in love with our ordinarily reclusive neighbor."

Lucy stared. "I haven't said—"

"You don't have to." Belle leaned forward and tugged the point of her chin. "It's written all over you. Just as Sarah described to Maggie, and Mags described to me."

"Grapevine," she muttered.

Belle's smile was sympathetic. "In this case, I'm grateful for it because at least I knew you weren't moping around any about that idiot, Lars." She waited a beat. "And I'm right, aren't I?"

Lucy exhaled. What was the point in pretending?

She nodded.

"So how serious has it gotten?"

"Serious. At least on my part." She chewed the inside of her lip. "Especially after last night."

"Ah," Belle murmured softly. "So what has you looking so upset the afternoon after?"

"He didn't show up this morning to work on the addition. And he didn't bring Shelby to dance. He said she had a fever and was taking her to the doctor, but—" she broke off and shook her head. "I think he's regretting what happened."

"Hmm." Belle pushed to her feet. "What do you plan to do about it?"

Lucy hugged her arms. She wasn't sure there was anything she could do about it. "It takes two willing people to make a relationship," she murmured. "I was going over to his house."

"Well, then." Belle gestured. "Go on over and see what's up."

"But you've just gotten home. I've barely even hugged Dad hello."

Belle waved her hands. "First off, we'll be here for a good long while." Her lips curved wryly. "*Right* here," she emphasized. "And just leave Cage to me." She scooped the keys off the counter and handed them to Lucy. "So go."

Even though she'd planned to do just that already, her hands still shook when she took the keys and went.

And when she got there, the sight of Beck's truck parked alongside his house didn't do a whole lot to alleviate the tension in her stomach.

She parked next to the truck and walked around the house to the front door.

She couldn't help but remember the day she'd brought the brownies and she had to sternly remind herself that they'd come a *long* way since that day. She curled her fist and rapped her knuckles on the massive door.

And just like that day that felt so long ago but really wasn't, he answered the door himself.

Then he'd worn jeans and a denim shirt, and today was no different. The only things missing were the cowboy hat and the grim expression.

The look on his face now just made her ache inside.

"How is Shelby?"

"Okay. She's sleeping."

Her mouth felt arid. She nodded. "Nothing serious, then?"

He shook his head.

"Okay, then." Her hands curled nervously. "What is it that you *can't* do?" Even as she asked the question, she knew it was moot.

She could see the answer on his face.

Read it in his bloodshot eyes.

"This. *Us*." His voice was low.

Final.

She thought she was prepared for the pain of it. Lord knows she'd told herself often enough to expect it.

But no amount of preparation was enough to withstand the blow of the real thing right there, up front and in her face

She wrapped her arms around her waist, holding herself together with a tenuous thread. "Can't, or won't?"

"It doesn't matter."

"It *does* matter," Lucy said huskily. She looked to either side of her at the sturdy, attractive porch furnishings. "After everything, you won't even invite me in?"

The door didn't budge. His muddy green eyes didn't flicker for even a moment. His resolve was steely. "I don't want Shelby waking up and getting even more upset."

"More," she repeated. "Which means she was already upset. Because you made a point of telling her I'm going back to New York?"

"It's true, isn't it? What else do you want me to say?"

Her arms unlocked from around her waist and she reached out to him but he caught her wrists before her hands could touch him. "Don't."

Her fingers curled into her fists. "Why not? Because it gets under your skin?" She yanked her hands free. "We both know that it does. We proved that last night. *Several* times."

A muscle in his jaw flexed. "I'm not denying that."

"Of course not. The sex was great."

He looked pained. "Lucy."

She wasn't even half finished, though. Not when the sharp pain inside her chest was driving her onward. "Don't call it what it was?" She leaned closer to him, lowering her voice. "We had S-E-X. You're a world-class lover, Beck. A really good—

"Enough," he barked. "Just because I can't be the man you deserve, doesn't mean you have to cut down making love with me."

There was a burning deep behind her eyes. "How very sensitive-sounding of you."

His eyes turned dark. He stepped out onto the porch and closed the door behind him none too gently. "Are you trying to provoke me?"

Lucy swallowed the knot in her chest but held her ground, staring up at him. "Would it do any good if I did?"

He exhaled roughly. "I shouldn't have touched you."

The burning was widening. *"Why?"*

"Because it's too complicated."

She shook her head. "It's only complicated if you want it to be."

"Shelby's way too attached to you."

"This isn't about Shelby and you know it." She was shaking but she still lifted her chin. "This is about you and me and the fact that I'm getting too close for your comfort." She swallowed hard and went for broke. "You know I'm in love with you and if you felt nothing for me in return, it probably wouldn't even bother you. But instead, you're getting cold feet because I'm crowding into the space you reserve only for Harmony!"

He was stock-still.

But he didn't deny it and her legs felt even more unsteady. "Beck." She had to stop and choke down the knot in her throat again. Only the rhythmic flexing in his jaw gave her the courage to stand there and not turn and run. "I'm not trying to push anyone out of your heart, least of all someone you've loved. I would never try to do that."

"It doesn't matter," he said again. "You're going back to New York."

Ask me to stay! Her nose burned. But all he did was look at her. She caught her lip between her teeth and gazed out over the beauty of the land surrounding the home he'd built. Here. In this area of the world. Only because it was the same area where his wife had been born.

"You know, I never thought I'd love anyone more than I loved ballet." Her voice was hoarse. "And it has nothing to do with my knee. Or some regret for what I've missed out on because of the choices I've made." She looked up at him. "I always thought I *had* to choose between one or the other." She blinked and a tear spilled over. But she was damned if she was going to be ashamed of them now. "But I was wrong. A heart's built to love. Period. And its walls are more expansive than I ever dreamed."

"I know what a heart can do." His voice sounded like gravel. "It made a decent man out of me when Harmony's heart decided on me."

The lump in her chest felt permanently lodged. "You *are* a good man. But do you honestly believe that her heart feels better knowing that you're never going to use *yours* again?" She looked into his eyes.

And her heart sank.

It didn't matter that she could see the regret there. Or the pain in the set of his jaw.

He wasn't going to change his mind.

Not now.

Not ever.

No amount of waiting was going to change that.

She drew in a shaking breath. "I didn't know Harmony. But I know you. And I *know* your daughter. And I know that's not what your wife would want." She drew in a shuddering breath. "You don't even have to love me, Beck. But I pray to God that someday, you let yourself love *someone*. Because that's something that would actually honor the woman and the life you shared." She leaned up and pressed her lips against his cheek. "At least it would if it had been me," she finished in a whisper.

Then she turned around and walked down the wide stairs of that lovely house.

She didn't look back.

She didn't count on the miniature bullet that streaked from the side of the house before she could reach the safe haven of her truck, and didn't even have time to swipe her wet cheeks before Shelby pelted against her, wrapping her arms around her waist, burying her face in her stomach.

"You can't leave," Shelby cried.

Lucy crouched down, hugging the girl close. She stroked her hand down Shelby's silky hair. "Baby, don't cry. It'll be all right."

"But Daddy says you're going back to New York."

Lucy closed her eyes. She pressed her cheek to the little girl's head. "I know he did," she whispered. "But even though they try really hard to, daddies sometimes don't know everything."

Shelby looked up at Lucy. Her eyes were gold and as shining as wet amber. "You're never gonna leave?"

"I can't say never," she said softly. "But I'm not going anywhere right now except home to the Lazy-B where my mom and dad are."

Shelby's breath hitched. "You're gonna come to my picnic at school?"

Could she ache any more deeply? "I promised you that I would, didn't I?"

Shelby nodded. "I *hate* Daddy. I told him so."

Lucy tucked her hand beneath Shelby's chin. "Don't do that," she said huskily. "Your daddy loves you more than anything in this world. He needs you to love him back just as much." She kissed Shelby's flushed nose. "And it wouldn't matter if I went back to New York or if I am here. I am *always* going to love you. Now." She turned Shelby around until she faced the side of the house. "Go back inside and tell your dad that you love him. You'll both feel better."

Shelby took a halting step but looked back, her expression pale and pinched. "You promise?"

"I promise."

"Shelby, eat your fried chicken." Beck tried to get his daughter to focus on the paper plate sitting on her lap rather than on the crowd milling around the playground.

It was the first day of school. "Real school" in Shelby's vernacular.

But the first day of "real school" was only a half day for the first through third graders and came along with the family picnic.

And his daughter was still too busy looking around her to eat what was on her plate.

All Beck wanted to do was get out of there and go home. It was hard enough being surrounded by screaming, excited children and their parents without constantly being reminded of Lucy. Everywhere he looked he saw something—or someone—who reminded him of her.

Lucy's red-haired cousin, Sarah, who taught third grade at the school and was doling out slices of sheet cake. Her old boyfriend and now cousin-in-law, Evan Taggart, who'd brought a bunch of baby piglets to show off. Even Jake and J.D. Forrest were there with two horses—one as beautiful as the finest thoroughbreds and one the saddest looking horse that Beck had ever seen. And then there were Shelby's friends who'd been taking Lucy's impromptu dance lessons and were twirling around as much as they were eating.

Even there, on his own blanket, with his own daughter, he was pelted with reminders. From Shelby, of course.

But also from Stan and Susan, who were sitting next to each other, poring over calendars and to-do lists as they talked nonstop wedding details.

It had been ten days since Lucy had walked off his porch. Ten days since she'd walked out of their lives.

Because he'd shoved her onto the path.

"Shelby. What are you waiting for? *Eat* your chicken."

She gave him an injured look. "I'm waiting for Lucy."

His jaw tightened. He ignored the look Stan gave him. "I told you. She's not coming." He'd finished the last of the trim work over at the Lazy-B last week. Lucy had been gone. He knew it because Cage had told him he'd taken her to the airport.

"She is too coming," Shelby insisted and crossed her arms dramatically. "She promised."

God help him.

"If you're not going to eat, then there's no point in staying."

She glared at him but picked up the crispy-coated drumstick and took a bite. And proceeded to chew so slowly that his patience thinned even more.

Then she dropped the piece of chicken and scrambled to her feet, the plate falling potato salad–side down on the blanket underneath them. "See?" She gave him an I-told-you-so look as she pointed. "There!" And she stomped away from him, the short ruffled skirt of her pink dress bouncing around her legs.

Beck looked and was almost afraid that he was seeing things. Because it *was* Lucy.

Looking like some sort of vision in a pale blue dress that floated around her slender ankles while her long, fair hair danced around her shoulders.

"Guess Shelby had more faith than you," Stan murmured beside him.

Beck glared.

His father lifted his hands, looking innocent. "Just saying."

Beck grimaced and looked toward Lucy again, only to realize she was carrying a stack of papers that she was distributing among the families there. She stopped the second Shelby caught up to her, though, and crouched down to open her arms for a hug.

Beck's chest ached. "What the hell's she doing here?" He looked at his father. Then at Susan. She was related to Lucy in a manner of speaking. "Do you know?"

Susan just shrugged, looking mildly amused. "Why don't you go ask her?"

"You're a big help," Beck muttered but without much heat. Because he really did like the woman. And then the point was moot because Shelby had Lucy's hand clutched in hers and they were both heading toward them.

Lucy didn't look at Beck, though. Instead, she greeted Stan and Susan, sounding warm and sincere. Then she stuck out one of the papers she was holding toward Beck. "I expect you to sign her up," was all she said.

Then, with a brilliant smile and wave, she turned and cheerfully greeted the family sitting next to Beck's. Shelby trotted after her, and Beck saw Lucy hand her a stack of the papers and nod. Shelby started skipping around the other attendees, distributing the papers herself.

He looked down at the page she'd shoved in his hand. It was a flyer, announcing the grand opening of Buchanan Ballet & Dance. He frowned and shoved the flyer at his father. "Did you know about this?"

Stan just gave him a look. "D'you think I wouldn't have mentioned it if I had? Maybe you'd have stopped stomping around like a bear with a sore paw."

His fingers crumpled the flyer as he strode after Lucy, catching up to her near the dessert table.

"I want to talk to you."

She glanced over her shoulder at him. Her eyes were as pale and blue and distinctive as ever, just the way they'd been haunting his every hour. "The schedule is on the flyer. Shelby would be in the beginner's class, obviously. You have three different days to choose from. Fill out the form today or later. You can mail or drop it off." She looked away from him and stopped in front of the dessert table. "Hey, Sarah. Can I have a piece?"

Her cousin's gaze went from Lucy to Beck. "Have as much as you like." She waved her hand over the cake. "We've got oodles left yet to get rid of."

Lucy transferred a slice to a napkin, looked at the flyers she still held, then pushed them into Beck's hand. "Hold these for a minute." She picked up her cake and scooped up a swirl of white-and-pale-green icing with the tip of her tongue before moving away, aiming for the swing set that was being ignored in favor of the horses the Forrests had brought.

His gut tight, he followed. "What sort of game are you playing?"

She raised an eyebrow as she settled herself on one of the swings. "You mean the swings?" She pressed one pointed toe of her sandals against the sandy ground, pushing herself back in the swing.

"*No*, I do not mean the *swings*."

She pointedly looked around him and set her swing moving again with her toe. "Watch your tone, Beck. There are children nearby."

He stepped in front of her and grabbed the chains, halting the slow arch. The swing jerkily stopped mid-swing, and her knees bumped his legs. "This game." He brandished the handful of flyers.

She gave a haughty sniff. "I really don't appreciate you calling my business a *game*."

It was a wonder she couldn't hear his teeth grinding. "Dammit, you *left*. Your father told me so!"

"I had a few things to tie up," she said coolly. "And now I'm back."

"To stay?"

For the first time, her gaze shied away from his. "My rates are reasonable," she said. "And for any children in Weaver who want to take a class but can't afford it, I've been able to set up a simple scholarship program, thanks to Jake. He suggested it. And will fund it for at least the first five years."

"Five *years?*" Beck nearly choked.

"That's what I said." She tucked the last small bite of cake in her mouth and delicately licked her fingertips before wiping them with the napkin. Then she jiggled the chains. "If you don't mind?"

"I do mind."

She looked pained. "I came from Weaver long before

you did, Beck. I have every right to move back and go into business if I want. I'm ready for new challenges." Then she hopped off the rubbery swing seat even though it meant bumping into him. "And it has nothing to do with you," she muttered as she slipped beneath his arm.

He caught her shoulder before she made it a foot. "I think it does."

She slowly looked from his hand up to his face. "As you've said to me often enough, it doesn't matter what you think. You may not be interested in moving on with your life, but I am. Now, if you'll excuse me–" she snatched the flyers out of his hand "—I want to get the rest of these passed out. I'm meeting a builder at the studio later this afternoon."

"Builder," he repeated stupidly, and watched her sashay away from him.

He was barely aware of his father coming up next to him until Stan spoke. "How many times are you going to let her walk away from you?"

Beck looked down at his hands. His wedding ring glinted in the sunlight. Shelby was still passing out flyers, oblivious to him. Susan had moved over to Jake and J.D. where they had the horses. "What if I lose her, too?"

"What if you don't?" Stan closed his hand over his shoulder and squeezed. "Son, if you don't go after her and tell her how you really feel, you're never going to have the chance to know."

Go on, now.

The voice—absent for so long—whispered through his head.

And he knew it would be the final time.

Harmony's work was finally done.

He let out a long breath.

And drew in a fresh one.

And went after his future.

"That wasn't so bad," Lucy murmured encouragingly to herself as she hurriedly crossed the street from the school to the town park. She'd survived the first encounter with Beck anyway. It had to get easier from here on out, didn't it?

She swiped her hands over her damp cheeks and swore as her foot caught the curb and she barely kept herself from pitching forward.

She laughed a little hysterically. It wouldn't do for her to fall and break something now, when she was actually excited about the new dance studio.

Even now, as she headed toward the pavilion in the park, she could see the glass-fronted building across the street. Down a few doors from Colbys. Up a few doors from Tara's shop, Classic Charms. It was on Main, a perfect location, and thanks to the investment that her father had insisted she accept she'd made an offer to purchase it—and the vacant space next to it—outright.

Now all she had to do was gut the interior, update the single bathroom, install floating floors and mirrors and barres and a sound system before the first class was scheduled in a month's time, and she'd be good to go. They could even do dance performances when the weather was nice in the pavilion.

"Assuming that you'll get the students," she said to herself.

"You'll get them."

She whirled.

Beck stood behind her, and she wondered if it would take the rest of her life before her heart would stop leaping just from the sight of him. "Are you following me?" She aimed for cool. Came off considerably *uncool,* considering how her voice shook.

"Yes."

She pressed her lips together for a moment and continued toward the pavilion. She wanted to see how badly the place needed painting because Belle had cautioned that it wasn't in such great repair any longer. "What do you want from me now?"

"Everything."

She went still. Caution screamed through her.

And he seemed to realize it because he sighed deeply as he moved in front of her. "Tell me honestly, Lucy. Am I one of the challenges you're willing to take on?"

Her heart felt in danger of stopping. "Why? Do you want another chance to throw it back in my face if I say that you are?"

"No." He held up his hand and pulled off his wedding ring.

She sank her teeth into her tongue. "You don't have to do that for me if, if that's what you think," she said shakily. "Your marriage is a part of you."

"It is. It was." He pushed the ring in the pocket of his jeans. "But I need to take it off for me because it's time for me to make room for something—some*one*—else."

She held her breath, too afraid to hope when he closed his arms around her shoulders.

"To make room for you," he finished in a low voice.

She sucked in a shaking breath. "Beck—"

His fingers pressed into her shoulders. "I need to say this."

"Because my brain has stopped functioning, that's fine," she said faintly.

The corner of his lips twitched. "Don't make me laugh. You can do that the rest of our lives, but not yet."

Her eyes flooded.

"I was never afraid of replacing Harmony," he said quietly. "I was afraid of losing again. So instead of grabbing on and holding tight when you danced into our lives, I pushed you away. I was doing exactly what you accused me of doing." His thumbs roved restlessly over her shoulders. "I was wrong."

"You were," she agreed faintly. "But I'm a forgiving sort."

His lips twitched again. "I'm probably going to have cause to remind you of that in the coming years."

"Years?"

His smile died. His gaze was serious as it seemed to bore into hers. "Years. Maybe you haven't noticed, but I'm an old-fashioned guy. I don't love lightly. And when I do it's for a lifetime."

Her knees would have gone out from beneath her if he hadn't been holding on to her. "You love me?"

"What did you think?"

She just shook her head, the tears finally slipping out of her control.

His hands slid from her shoulders to cup her face. His thumbs stroked away the tears. "I love you, Lucy Buchanan. So I'll ask one more time. Am I one of those challenges?"

She let out a shaking laugh, finally daring to believe. "You'll be the best challenge of them all."

He exhaled, his eyes closing for a moment. "Thank you." Then he pressed his lips slowly to hers.

Lucy twined her arms around him and held on. "I'm afraid I'll wake up and this will all be a dream."

He lifted his head. "No dream," he assured deeply. "This is life. Our life."

Her heart spilled over, just as surely as her eyes had. "I do love you, Beck."

He took her hands in his and kissed them. "I love you." Then he smiled a little crookedly and his eyes glinted. "So what do you think Shelby is going to say about having a ballerina join the family?"

Lucy's laughter filled the air and it was a sound Beck knew he'd never tire of. She tangled her fingers in his and tugged. "Former ballerina. And there's only one sure way to find out…"

Epilogue

The bride wore white and looked radiant with her hair pulled back in a smooth chignon with a peony tucked alongside.

The groom wore a black suit and looked handsome and thoroughly besotted with his bride as he watched her walk down the aisle.

Their vows were spoken clearly and truly in front of the minister in the little Weaver church that had seen so many marriages begin there.

And as the newly wedded couple recessed along the aisle, the guests clapped and cheered and followed them out into the bright sunlight that glittered off the fresh layer of snow that had fallen overnight.

Lucy looped her hand through Beck's arm and pressed her cheek to his shoulder as they followed his father and his brand-new bride out of the church. "Happy?"

"I will be when I get out of this tie," he murmured, smiling a little as he reached for the knot in question.

She swatted his hand away. "Don't mess up your tie. You've still got pictures."

He wrapped his arm around her waist and regardless of the guests milling around them, pulled her close for a kiss. "I don't care about the pictures."

"I do," she whispered, and lightly nipped his lip. "Shelby looks like a princess in her dress."

They both looked over to where Beck's daughter was preening near the wedding photographer and her grandfather-the-groom. Lucy had braided Shelby's hair down the back of her head, weaving baby's breath among the silky, dark strands and the pale blue dress she wore had puffy sleeves and miles of lace and frills. "I want as many pictures of her as we can get," she added. "Because there's going to come a day, I promise you, when she'll positively *moan* over ever having worn all those ruffles."

"You didn't get tired of ruffles," he pointed out, grinning. "That sexy little thing you wore last night had a ruffle right over your—"

She covered his mouth. "We're at a church here," she whispered.

"And remind me again how glad I am that we decided to forgo all the hoopla." He caught her fingers in his and pressed a kiss to the platinum diamond-studded wedding band surrounding her finger. "We moved right on to the honeymoon."

Which was still going on, as far as Lucy was concerned. They'd been married a little over a month now after a simple ceremony with just her family and his present one afternoon in their living room, and not a day went by that wasn't filled with some fresh joy.

Oh, they'd had arguments plenty already. From the interior layout of the dance studio which Beck insisted on handling, even though she'd initially planned for her uncle Daniel to do the simple job.

Lucy had won out on the design she wanted, though, and she had it on good authority from her grandmother that Daniel was perfectly happy *not* to have the work because he was enjoying his retirement and his latest new grandbaby too much. But she could certainly admit to her handsome husband now that she'd had classes running for nearly three months, that some of the things he'd insisted upon had been good ideas. Like more than one bathroom.

He still insisted that she was putting in too many hours, but the classes were only enough to keep her busy part-time, so that was another argument he'd been doomed to lose.

For now, she thought to herself. For now.

"Beck." Stan, the bridegroom, beckoned his best man over. "Get your hide over here for pictures."

Lucy nudged him along. She wasn't officially in the wedding party. Jake's two sisters had arrived to see their aunt get married and had stood up with Susan, while Beck and Nick had stood up for Stan. And standing in the center of them was the grinning princess, Shelby.

"That's quite a family we've got," J.D. murmured, coming up beside Lucy. "Have you told him yet?"

Lucy rested her palm over her flat tummy. "I will at the reception. I didn't want anything taking away from Stan and Susan's wedding day."

"I'm pretty sure Beck's not going to think of this as taking away from anything," J.D. said with a laugh. "But my lips are sealed, as promised."

"Thanks."

J.D. winked. "I should be thanking you. I know we have you to thank for Beck agreeing to design the buildings for Crossing West."

Lucy shook her head. "He would have agreed eventually."

"Well, now we can get the drawings and the permits all done before we break ground in the spring," J.D. said. "So I'm a happy lady."

So was Lucy.

A happy, married, pregnant lady.

She couldn't wait to tell Beck.

And just as the photographer laughed and called it quits, and the wedding party scattered, everyone heading in the general direction of the parking lot and Beck and Lucy's house where the caterer they'd hired had been setting up for the past two days, Lucy heard a faint voice.

Go on, now.

She looked around at J.D. "Did you say something?"

J.D. gave her a strange look. "Nope."

Lucy shook her head slightly. Maybe pregnancy hormones had already started to cause voices in her head.

Go on. Now, the voice insisted. A woman's voice.

And suddenly, Lucy realized.

She smiled slightly, and lowered her hand from her belly. And she went up to Beck and tugged his head down. She whispered in his ear.

His head shot up. He gave her a sharp look. "Really?"

"Mallory called to confirm it this morning."

The smile grew slowly. Until it lit his entire face. He wrapped his arms around her and picked her right off her feet, swinging her around.

And he laughed.

* * * * *

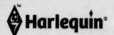
Harlequin®

COMING NEXT MONTH

Available April 26, 2011

#2113 COWBOY, TAKE ME AWAY
Kathleen Eagle

#2114 FORTUNE'S SECRET BABY
Christyne Butler
The Fortunes of Texas: Lost...and Found

#2115 THE PRINCE'S TEXAS BRIDE
Leanne Banks

#2116 THE VIRGIN AND ZACH COULTER
Lois Faye Dyer
Big Sky Brothers

#2117 A MATCH FOR THE DOCTOR
Marie Ferrarella
Matchmaking Mamas

#2118 HUSBAND FOR HIRE
Susan Crosby
Wives for Hire

SPECIAL EDITION

HSECNM0411

REQUEST YOUR FREE BOOKS!

2 FREE NOVELS PLUS 2 FREE GIFTS!

✦Harlequin®

SPECIAL EDITION

Life, Love & Family

YES! Please send me 2 FREE Harlequin Special Edition® novels and my 2 FREE gifts (gifts are worth about $10). After receiving them, if I don't wish to receive any more books, I can return the shipping statement marked "cancel." If I don't cancel, I will receive 6 brand-new novels every month and be billed just $4.24 per book in the U.S. or $4.99 per book in Canada. That's a saving of at least 15% off the cover price! It's quite a bargain! Shipping and handling is just 50¢ per book in the U.S. and 75¢ per book in Canada.* I understand that accepting the 2 free books and gifts places me under no obligation to buy anything. I can always return a shipment and cancel at any time. Even if I never buy another book, the two free books and gifts are mine to keep forever.

235/335 SDN FC7H

Name	(PLEASE PRINT)	
Address		Apt. #
City	State/Prov.	Zip/Postal Code

Signature (if under 18, a parent or guardian must sign)

Mail to the **Reader Service:**
IN U.S.A.: P.O. Box 1867, Buffalo, NY 14240-1867
IN CANADA: P.O. Box 609, Fort Erie, Ontario L2A 5X3

Not valid for current subscribers to Harlequin Special Edition books.

Want to try two free books from another line?
Call 1-800-873-8635 or visit www.ReaderService.com.

* Terms and prices subject to change without notice. Prices do not include applicable taxes. Sales tax applicable in N.Y. Canadian residents will be charged applicable taxes. Offer not valid in Quebec. This offer is limited to one order per household. All orders subject to credit approval. Credit or debit balances in a customer's account(s) may be offset by any other outstanding balance owed by or to the customer. Please allow 4 to 6 weeks for delivery. Offer available while quantities last.

Your Privacy—The Reader Service is committed to protecting your privacy. Our Privacy Policy is available online at www.ReaderService.com or upon request from the Reader Service.

We make a portion of our mailing list available to reputable third parties that offer products we believe may interest you. If you prefer that we not exchange your name with third parties, or if you wish to clarify or modify your communication preferences, please visit us at www.ReaderService.com/consumerschoice or write to us at Reader Service Preference Service, P.O. Box 9062, Buffalo, NY 14269. Include your complete name and address.

*With an evil force hell-bent on destruction,
two enemies must unite to find a truth that turns
all-too-personal when passions collide.*

*Enjoy a sneak peek in Jenna Kernan's next installment
in her original* TRACKER *series,* GHOST STALKER,
available in May, only from Harlequin Nocturne.

"**W**ho are you?" he snarled.

Jessie lifted her chin. "Your better."

His smile was cold. "Such arrogance could only come from a Niyanoka."

She nodded. "Why are you here?"

"I don't know." He glanced about her room. "I asked the birds to take me to a healer."

"And they have done so. Is that *all* you asked?"

"No. To lead them away from my friends." His eyes fluttered and she saw them roll over white.

Jessie straightened, preparing to flee, but he roused himself and mastered the momentary weakness. His eyes snapped open, locking on her.

Her heart hammered as she inched back.

"Lead who away?" she whispered, suddenly afraid of the answer.

"The ghosts. Nagi sent them to attack me so I would bring them to her."

The wolf must be deranged because Nagi did not send ghosts to attack living creatures. He captured the evil ones after their death if they refused to walk the Way of Souls, forcing them to face judgment.

"Her? The healer you seek is also female?"

"Michaela. She's Niyanoka, like you. The last Seer of Souls and Nagi wants her dead."

Jessie fell back to her seat on the carpet as the possibility of this ricocheted in her brain. Could it be true?

"Why should I believe you?" But she knew why. His black aura, the part that said he had been touched by death. Only a ghost could do that. But it made no sense.

Why would Nagi hunt one of her people and why would a Skinwalker want to protect her? She had been trained from birth to hate the Skinwalkers, to consider them a threat.

His intent blue eyes pinned her. Jessie felt her mouth go dry as she considered the impossible. Could the trickster be speaking the truth? Great Mystery, what evil was this?

She stared in astonishment. There was only one way to find her answers. But she had never even met a Skinwalker before and so did not even know if they dreamed.

But if he dreamed, she would have her chance to learn the truth.

Look for GHOST STALKER by Jenna Kernan,
available May only from Harlequin Nocturne,
wherever books and ebooks are sold.

HNEXP0511